D1530799

Meet Me at the
BOARDWALK

ERIN HAFT

Point

No part of this publication may be reproduced, stored in a retrieval system, or transmitted in any
form or by any means, electronic, mechanical, photocopying, recording, or otherwise, without
written permission of the publisher.
For information regarding permission, write to Scholastic Inc., Attention: Permissions
Department, 557 Broadway, New York, NY 10012.

ISBN-13: 978-0-545-04213-0
ISBN-10: 0-545-04213-5

12 11 10 9 8 7 6 5 4 3 2 1   8 9 10 11 12 13/0
Printed in the U.S.A.
First Scholastic printing, May 2008

To Aimee Friedman,
the one who fixes what might
have been torn down.

Plans in the Works to Destroy

MAY 27, 7:15 A.M.
FROM THE EDITOR

Citizens! We may be facing the biggest crisis ever in the history of Seashell Point.

This is no joke. We do a lot of joking on this page. Not this time. Tragically, due to circumstances beyond our control, we've been forced to be serious for once.

For decades, our resort town has earned its reputation — and revenue — on juicy summer fun. To paraphrase *Us Weekly*, "Seashell Point's mile-long strip of beachfront mansions provides the premier summer retreat for the East Coast jet set." We've never apologized for it. We shouldn't. Think of the celebrity sightings, the sunrises, the surfing . . . and, why not, the scandal. Rejoice in it! How about last season, when a certain famous news anchor was videotaped frolicking on his boat with a certain famous musician's wife. Remember that? It set a new YouTube record for most hits.

AND — note that we have the decency not to provide the link here.

That speaks to our values. We're protective. And yes, that still goes if you're here for one summer only — for a fling or an affair. You're still a part of our community. Your outrageous behavior defines us, as much as our five-star clams, the cobbled streets of downtown — and perhaps most important

Our Most Treasured Landmark!

LATE EDITION BREAKING NEWS

of all, our ninety-year-old boardwalk.

Ninety years. Think about that. Our boardwalk is older than the state of Hawaii! We mention this because several professional surfers prefer the conditions at Seashell Point to those at Maui. We've researched. We also discovered our town is the number-one "mistress hideaway" in all of Maryland, but that's another story. . . .

Now think about what it would mean if the boardwalk were to be torn down. No more two-dollar buckets of fried clams at Sonny's Clam Shack. No more Pete's Petting Zoo. No more Amusement Alley. Can you imagine Paris without the Eiffel Tower? Hollywood without its eponymous sign in the hills? St. Louis without the Arch?

Hyperbole? Maybe. But the boardwalk *is* Seashell Point.

And we fear that tearing it down is exactly what real-estate mogul Arnold Roth intends to do. Worse, he may be acting with the help of our very own tourist board president and town council chairwoman, Suzanne Kim. Though Ms. Kim will neither confirm nor deny Mr. Roth's intentions, she did agree to meet with us on the boardwalk early this morning.

Her teenage daughter, Megan, tagged along.

"All I know for certain is that Mr. Roth plans to enjoy the best of Seashell Point, like any other tourist," Ms. Kim told us. "He's vacationing here for the summer with his wife, Cheryl, and daughter, Lily-Ann. They picked a very nice six-bedroom on the south side, formerly rented by some of the Sean 'Diddy' Combs entourage."

And how did you come to learn this information? You don't work in real estate.

"Mr. Roth visited last summer for a weekend to get a look at the house, and he dropped by the tourist board office, mostly to tell us how much he loves our town. We did discuss some ideas he had about urban revitalization. That's all I have to say."

No more? Really? That's ALL?

Ms. Kim clasped her daughter's hand. "No, that's not all. My daughter, as you know, cleans tourist homes during the summer. She decided to do this on her own two years ago, as a way to earn spending money. She'll be cleaning Mr. Roth's house. Why she does this instead of working with me at the tourist board or city council is frankly a mystery, but I admire her work ethic."

"It isn't a mystery," Megan clarified. "Jade got me the job. And I like it."

"Right, that would be Jade Cohen," Ms. Kim continued, in a somewhat different tone. "The local yoga instructor's daughter, who was fired for negligence and now sells tickets for the Jupiter Bounce at Amusement Alley. The point is: If I had any doubts about

Mr. Roth's character, I certainly wouldn't allow my daughter to work for him."

The younger Ms. Kim declined further comment.

We asked the elder Ms. Kim point-blank: *What about your character? Do YOU want to tear down the boardwalk? And what would you put up in its place?*

"I've loved and served Seashell Point my entire life," she said. "But the boardwalk can encourage destructive behavior. Take the Jupiter Bounce — toddlers have suffered bumps and bruises. And this may sound alarmist, but tourists tend to gather on the boardwalk to cheer the surfers. The riskier the surfing, the louder the cheers. Last summer, a local boy and a dear friend of my daughter's was hospitalized after a surfing accident. I'm not trying to discourage surfing if it's done responsibly — and I'm not saying that surfing shouldn't be a spectator sport, either. I just don't want to jeopardize the safety of our citizens."

With that cryptic nonanswer, Ms. Kim ended the interview.

Shakespeare once said, "Something is rotten in the state of Denmark."

Indeed. Something is rotten in Seashell Point, people. Don't let them take our beloved boardwalk from us! It's time to fight back!

Part One
The Pact

Jade

There's a certain moment in your life when you realize something. It's along the lines of: Hey, you *aren't* a kid anymore. You might actually have to start worrying about lame grown-up sorts of stuff — like how to repair a screen door, or where to find the right scented candle to repel beach bugs, or the best way to avoid a wicked older sister. (Or how to finagle getting whisked off forever by a skinny, brilliant, gorgeous rock star. Though I wouldn't call that a grown-up concern per se.)

Personally, I prefer to worry about which one-piece bathing suit will magically make me appear taller than an elf. And serve as a natural aphrodisiac. I have yet to find it. In my defense, though, most of the high-end stores in town are out of my price range.

Anyway, this moment of grown-up realization came for me when Dad dropped what I call the SF bomb.

I don't know about other people's dads, but my dad is a freak.

He *calls* himself a freak and he means it in a good way. Apparently when he was my age back in the sixties, calling someone a "freak" was a compliment. I have no way of verifying this — my two best friends' parents are much younger than Dad. Still, I'll take his word for the definition. He may be many things: an aging hippie, a yoga instructor, a grizzled free spirit who nags his youngest daughter for obsessing over bathing suits . . . but he is honest to a fault. Honesty = good. Gray beard, poncho, and thinning ponytail = bad.

Dad dropped the SF Bomb at six A.M. the Tuesday morning after Memorial Day. I mention the time and date because in other towns, it might not mean much: The beginning of a short week, at most. But in Seashell Point, that Tuesday is the day the "season" officially begins. Over Memorial Day weekend, the population of our quaint little beachside dump nearly triples. (Whoops. Did I say "dump"? I meant "resort town." I really did.) In they roar, like a herd of stampeding elephants, the Mercedes and Range Rovers and Jaguar convertibles . . . a massive amount of disposable incomes (whoops, tourists), who all believe that it's glamorous to spend a summer of surf and sun in a quaint little Maryland . . . um . . . resort town. Right.

My best friends, Miles Gordon and Megan Kim, and I have practically made a career out of making fun of them.

First Tuesday of the season or not, Dad wakes up at sunrise every morning to practice yoga by the water. When it's warm enough, I'll join him. Not for yoga (*blech*), but to dive into the ocean for a quick cold dip. We have our routine: The back screen door of our bungalow opens directly onto the beach, and if I run fast enough, I can splash into the water literally ten seconds after racing outside.

That morning, as usual, I broke into a sprint, until I heard, "Jade, sweetie, wait!"

I stopped and turned. "What's up?"

Dad tightened the yoga mat in his hands. He kneaded the foam anxiously — as if it were a giant rolled-up newspaper and he'd just read some bad news.

"Are you okay?" I asked.

"Yeah . . . there's just — something I have to tell you." He stepped out into the moist sand and laid the mat at my feet. "Here. Sit with me."

"This isn't about a towel, is it, Dad?" I asked, sitting beside him. "I'm not gonna catch pneumonia or anything. I'm just gonna run right in and run right back —"

"No, Jade," he interrupted quietly. "You know how to take care of yourself."

He turned toward the ocean, his green eyes — exactly like mine — pensive. Dawn was just starting to break, with the faintest glimmer of orange-red sun over the waves. Okay, I have to admit it: At this time of day, in this spot, Seashell Point can be pretty beautiful. I can almost understand — at least for five minutes, until the fog starts to burn off — how tourists might want to come here every year in droves.

"It really is beautiful, isn't it?" Dad murmured.

I laughed.

"What?" he said.

"Nothing. Except that for once I was thinking the exact same thing as you were."

He bit his lip. "Jade, I got an e-mail last night."

"You know how to use our computer?" I joked.

He chuckled, his eyes still glued to the ocean. "I'm gonna miss your sass."

"Dad, you're freaking me out a little here. And not 'freak' in a good way. What's wrong? Why would you miss my sass?"

"I . . ." He took a deep breath and turned back to me. "I got a job offer. In San Francisco. A really sweet gig. Teaching yoga at a private studio until Labor Day. I'll be able to run my own workshops and earn about three times what I make here. I'm going to put the extra earnings in a college fund for you."

My eyes widened. "Are you serious?"

"Absolutely."

I'm not a terribly emotive person — at least not with physical displays. But I threw my arms around Dad. I couldn't help it. I probably hadn't hugged him since his birthday.

The truth is, though, I was mostly happy for me.

"Dad, that is so cool!" I exclaimed. "You know I've always wanted to get out of here during the summer. Well, get out of here, period, and I've always wanted to see the West Coast. Maybe we can even convince Megan and Miles to come visit. . . ." My jabbering trailed off, though, and I pulled away. "Wait. You're not telling me the whole story, are you?"

He shook his head, silent.

"I can't come with you. Is that it? That's why you're gonna miss my sass?"

"Jade, I'm sorry." He tugged at his beard. "It wasn't fair of me. I fought really hard with the owners of the studio to let me stay off-premises. I wanted to rent an apartment with you, but they have a single residence on-site. It's legally 'one occupant only' and —"

"No, no." I cut him off and held up my hands, swallowing. "No worries. I'm serious. I'm happy for you." I fought to believe the words as I said them. "I know you love San Francisco, too." I mustered a smile. "Just please don't tell me that I have to spend the summer with Nana in Boca Raton. It's possibly the only place on Earth that's worse than Seashell Point."

"No, you won't have to spend the summer in Boca. But I might ask Nana to come up here and check in on you once or twice."

The disappointment began to fade. My lips curled in a grin. "What are you saying? That I can stay here alone?"

A rapid-fire montage of wild summer scenes flashed through my head: themed parties, barbecues, boardwalk protests against the tourists (except the cute boys) . . . all starring me, Megan, and Miles. Maybe I'd even get to kiss a hot tourist, and even better if he played in a band —

"Not exactly alone," Dad said.

Uh-oh.

"Turquoise will be staying here, too."

"What?"

Dad placed his hand on my arm. "Jade, this could be a time for you and your sister to bond. I've given this a lot of thought. And I'm sorry to have kept you in the dark for so long. But you know, sweetie, you and Turquoise are not as unalike as you think."

"But what about her job in New York?" I practically yelled. "I thought she landed some cushy internship at a law firm with all her Ivy League buddies!"

"She decided to skip it and study hard for the bar exam instead. As crazy as this may sound to you, she also wanted to spend some time with her little sister."

I sniffed. "Right. So she can shove my nose into the fact that she's so brilliant, and I'm nothing more than — and I'm quoting her here, I swear — a 'dwarfish emo chick.' Yes, Dad. We're absolutely alike. I'm human. She is evil incarnate."

He laughed.

"I assume you're laughing at my sass," I grumbled.

Dad patted my foot. "Thanks for understanding. And I, for one, am pretty thrilled that 'evil incarnate' will be spending the summer with you. She's flying into DC tonight. She's renting a car and getting in late."

"Wonderful," I mumbled.

The fog was starting to break. The sun grew hotter. I wasn't so much in the mood to take a dip. Or go to school later. All I wanted to do was to crawl back into bed. Which, of course, was why I was the one who needed the college fund — and why Turquoise didn't. Turquoise had earned a full scholarship with her 1600 SATs and 4.0 GPA and more extracurricular activities than Seashell Point High even offered. (I'm serious. She *brought* the Model U.N. *to* school. It was even written up in *The Seashell Register*: "LOCAL GENIUS TRUMPS DUMB YOUNGER SISTER AGAIN!" Okay, the headline was different, but I prefer mine.)

"But seriously, Jade, listen up," Dad said. "Later today, after school, there are some things we need to go over. The screen door is a little wobbly these days, but the shop over on Chesapeake Street has all the stuff you need to repair it. And you know those insect-repelling scented candles? If you and Turquoise want to barbecue this summer, use a different brand, the ones in those big buckets. We had some mosquito trouble last year and I want . . ."

Dad might have kept talking. I wasn't sure. He could talk all the way to San Francisco, as far as I was concerned. Because I was on my way, too — across the sand and back into the house . . . making a point to slam the screen door extra hard, so that it rattled in its frame and cracked back open a little, just enough to let the beach bugs in.

Megan

Jade is always telling me that I'm too shy and quiet. I guess I am. But keeping quiet works for me. Not that there isn't lots I want to say. There are just plenty of things that I need to keep to myself. Because when I get nervous, I tend to blurt.

I shouldn't have been nervous. I don't know why I was nervous. Actually, that's not true: I know exactly why I was nervous.

I was about to see Miles.

Confession: I have been secretly in love with my best friend, Miles Gordon, for most of my life.

So I get nervous every morning.

Every single morning before school, since the very first day of third grade, Jade, Miles, and I have met at the exact same spot on the boardwalk. The spot on which I now stood, a knot in my stomach and the wind whipping my jet-black hair.

This tradition started the way I imagine most traditions start: by accident. Nine-year-old Jade and I had bumped into each other on the beach. We were both collecting shells for show-and-tell. Jade had wandered off from her dad (he was practicing yoga), and I'd wandered off from my mom (she was schmoozing with some tourist) . . . and we both zeroed in on the same conch shell at the exact same time.

Two things that bear mentioning: We were already best friends at this point and we were also in a fight. Neither of us can remember what the fight was about. That's generally been the case with us.

"Megan?" Jade had said.

"Jade?" I had said.

"Do you want that conch for show-and-tell?" Jade demanded.

"Yes," I admitted.

She opened her mouth, but before she could answer, a boy with the blondest hair you could ever imagine scampered in out of nowhere and grabbed the shell. I vaguely recognized him from school.

"Hey!" Jade yelled. "We wanted that!"

He paused in the sand, grinning at us. "Finders keepers."

Jade put her hands on her hips. "That's the best you can come up with?"

"Well, no . . . but you wanted it for show-and-tell, right?" he asked.

Jade nodded. "Yeah. So?"

He marched over to Jade. "Sorry," he murmured.

Jade and I gaped at him. Then we gaped at each other. Neither of us had ever heard a boy say "sorry" before. We were nine. We'd heard boys say "booger" and "wiener," and that was pretty much it.

Miles pointed at the boardwalk. "I'll make you a deal. If you two meet me right there every day before school, I'll let you have this conch shell."

"Why would we want to meet you before school?" Jade asked.

"I don't have any brothers or sisters," he replied simply. "Usually you go to school with a brother or sister, right?"

"Wrong," Jade replied. "I mean — depending on the sister. But, okay, you have a deal." She stuck out her hand.

He handed her the shell.

And then Jade handed the shell to me.

Every school day since then, we've met at the exact spot Miles pointed to on the boardwalk.

Thanks to Mom's lame and awful interview, I was way more dressed-up than on a typical last-week-of-school day: a Swiss-dot strapless sundress, patent leather ballet flats . . . the works. Also, I knew that Miles had read the article. Ever since the accident, he's always read the paper. He says it's "distracting." The fact that Mom used his accident to prove a point about tearing down the boardwalk made me want to send *her* to the hospital. Miles's accident had nothing to do with people cheering. It was a fluke.

The boardwalk isn't exactly crowded at nine A.M. on Tuesday after Memorial Day. When the sun clears the fog, it's just a gaggle of old surfers and vendors. On the first day of the season, the tourists all sleep in. It's another Seashell Point tradition, even for those who don't *know* the tradition. I've always loved that. It's as if there's this big, unspoken, psychic connection.

I was dwelling on that when I noticed Jade. She looked as she always did. Dark and petite, she was wearing denim cut-offs and flip-flops. But today, she looked mighty pissed.

"Ugh!" she shouted. "Ugh! Ugh! Ugh!"

"What?" I cried, wondering if *she'd* seen the article.

"This summer is going to be a nightmare!"

Jade

"Why?" Megan asked, looking understandably concerned. "Because of the whole boardwalk —"

"Guess who's coming to town?" I cut in.

Megan shrugged. "My mom would know. Angelina Jolie?"

I almost smiled. "Turkey. And you know why?" I leaned over the rickety wooden railing and scowled at the surfers, then yanked my sunglasses out of my bag and shoved them on. "Because Dad is going to spend all summer in San Francisco, and he wants Turkey and me to 'bond.'" I made air quotes around the word, imitating Dad's gravelly voice. "She's coming here to take time off to study for the bar exam. We'll be alone all summer together. Turkey!"

Megan, as usual, was silent.

I started calling my older sister Turkey when Megan and I were four and Turquoise was nine. Needless to say, Turquoise hates it — which is also the reason of course why I will never, ever, ever stop calling her Turkey.

I peered at Megan over the rims of my sunglasses. Megan is tall and porcelain and drop-dead gorgeous. In Seashell Point, she stands out in a good way, since most of us locals tend to get wrinkled and tanned even in the dead of winter. But when Megan was little, her height and coloring weren't exactly pluses, especially not with insecure turds — i.e., 99 percent of the year-round kids in our town — ragging on her.

"Hey, what's with the fancy threads?" I asked. "*Is* Angelina Jolie coming here this summer?"

She tried to laugh. "My mom had this interview with *The Seashell Register* this morning, and she dragged me along. It's not worth even getting into."

"Is everything okay?" I asked.

"Totally," she lied. She is by far the lousiest liar on the planet. "So why is your dad going to spend all summer in San Francisco?" she asked.

I decided not to pry. She wouldn't have told me what was wrong, anyway. "He got a yoga-teaching gig," I said.

"Really? That's so awesome!" she exclaimed. "You can turn your bungalow into a big Seashell Point party house. I mean, really: Turquoise is probably going to spend all her time at the library, anyway, buried in law books. It'll be like a vacation in your own home. It'll be like *you're* a tourist!"

I removed my sunglasses. "Are you on drugs?"

She sighed with a little smirk. "No, it's just that . . . when I'm —"

"Nervous, you tend to blurt." I squeezed her arm. "I know. What's up?"

She turned back toward the water and drummed her fingers on the railing. I knew she wasn't going to speak.

"You know what, Megan, you are totally right," I said instead.

"About what?"

"About turning my house into a party house. About living like a tourist! I mean it's funny because I had that same exact idea, too, before I found out that Turkey would be coming. Seriously, Meg. Not to get all corny on you, but this is our last summer before senior year. We have to make the most of it. Think about how many times we've stood in this exact spot and wondered what it would be like to live like a tourist. Now we have the upper hand. *We'll* have the crazy parties. You and me and Miles! But — wait. Okay. We have to make sure you and I are the only girls. Well, maybe not the *only* girls, but we'll make sure that no other super-hot chicks come except you. And tons of yummy tourist boys. Ha! I love it!"

Megan swallowed. "See? I shouldn't have opened my mouth," she murmured.

I stared at her. Something really *was* bothering her. I knew it wasn't the usual, either: that I needed to stop harping on how beautiful she was. But why shouldn't I harp? When she talks about herself (almost never) in a fit of verbosity, it's along the lines of: *"Thin, black-haired, milk-pale, and Asian? That may work for Manga or some Japanese Goth fashion magazine, but it has never worked in Seashell Point."*

I decided to wait to let her speak.

What finally came out of Meg's mouth was: "You'd hook up with a tourist?"

I rolled my eyes. "Please, Meg. If he were a rock star, yes. Anyway, *you* got with Sean Edwards."

Her face flushed. "I . . . did — I did not 'get' with Sean Edwards," she stammered, but then she laughed out loud.

"Don't try to con a con artist," I said drily. "I saw you guys. Amusement Alley. Two summers ago. You took the little kiddie ride through the haunted house. When you went in, he had his arm around you. When the car came out, you two were sucking face."

"I . . . I . . ." she sputtered. "I only kissed him because —"

"Hey! It's okay. We all make mistakes. And Sean *is* pretty cute."

"But he's a moron!" she exclaimed.

"Sure, he's not that much smarter than the animatronic ghosts inside the haunted house, but those blue eyes are to die for."

"Exactly!" She sighed and shook her head. "Jeez. It's the blurting thing again."

"I'll take that as a confession." I chuckled to myself, and then dug into my bag. "Here, you look a little red. Put some sunblock on. What time was your big newspaper interview? You've probably been standing in the sun for hours now."

"Thanks, Dad," she said.

"You're welcome, Mom."

She stifled a laugh — then she grabbed the bottle of 45-SPF out of my hands. I only carried it around for her. Every summer, it always happens: She forgets to wear sunblock one day and ends up lobster-red. Her real mom, unfortunately, is always just a tad more concerned with how her daughter's sunburn will affect the tourist trade. *"Honey, you don't need to stop by the office after work; I have clients. You might want to call the Who's-Its and warn them about your appearance in case they have guests."*

These are actual quotes.

"You know what the funny thing is," Megan said, handing back the lotion. "I think I will actually have to be your dad this summer."

"Hey, I'm fine. If I need any male guidance, there's always Miles."

She opened her mouth, and then closed it.

"What?" I felt an unpleasant stirring inside.

"No, you're right," she said in a faraway voice. "There's always Miles."

For once, I decided to remain silent. I have always, always suspected that Megan harbored a crush on Miles. But I couldn't see the two of them together. They were like siblings. We all were.

Which made me feel that much worse about what had happened last summer.

At the exact same moment, I spotted a tall blond boy down the boardwalk. A boy with sinewy tanned arms, bright brown eyes, and a slight limp — a surfer who no longer surfed — smiling and hobbling toward us as fast as he could, as he had every morning before school this year. Miles Gordon, the boy with whom I shared a terrible, awful secret.

Megan

"**I** want to be a giraffe."

That was when he had me. At that moment, I knew I would marry him.

We were both nine years old, but still — I knew. It was fourth grade. Our homeroom teacher, Mr. Browning, had just posed the question "What do you want to be when you grow up?" The way Mr. Browning kept yawning and rubbing his bleary eyes . . . well, I doubted he'd spent the previous afternoon preparing a lesson plan. Actually, I knew for a fact that he'd spent the afternoon surfing. Surfers here tend to relax after a hard day . . . and not by thinking about class. He was winging it.

His tired gaze swept over us. "Megan Kim?" he asked.

"Mayor of Seashell Point," I answered quietly.

Everybody laughed.

"What? It would be fun." I was blushing furiously.

"Dorks can have *fun*?" Brian Ashe hooted from the back.

Jade spun around in her chair. "What do you want to be, Brian, the village idiot?"

Brian Ashe is still the biggest idiot in Seashell Point — even bigger than the worst summer tourist — and with each passing day, he bears a closer resemblance to Cletus, the slack-jawed yokel from *The Simpsons*.

All the other boys started cracking up, including Miles.

23

"Okay, class. Settle down," Mr. Browning grumbled. "How about you, Jade? What do you want to be when you grow up?"

She shrugged.

But a few other kids were still snickering at me, and I was cringing, and before Jade could think of an answer, Miles chimed in with: "I want to be a giraffe."

The classroom fell silent. No more snickers.

Then I started laughing. Nobody laughed but me.

I clamped my hand over my mouth. Miles grinned back. My hand fell away. I remember how his eyes (think caramel brown), softened then, sort of a glimpse into the way he looks now. He brushed his blond hair out of his face and jammed his hands into his shorts pockets, and then started to talk, the whole time he stared at me instead of Mr. Browning.

"No, really," he said. "Giraffes can grab fruit out of trees that no person can reach. Or what about all those game stands on the boardwalk? How they have to use that stick-and-claw thingy to get the prizes on the high shelves? A giraffe could do that. Plus, a giraffe would be the coolest animal at Pete's Petting Zoo. That's where I would be —"

"That's very nice, Miles," Mr. Browning interrupted. "But the question was directed at Jade. Jade Cohen? Care to respond?"

"President of the I-Hate-Brian-Ashe Club," she said.

Everybody laughed again. My hand shot up.

"Megan, I see you'd like to add to this discussion." Mr. Browning groaned.

"No, but I changed my mind," I announced. "I want to be boss of Pete's Petting Zoo. I can work my way up to mayor from there. Jade will be my deputy."

Oh, and if the giraffe thing doesn't work out for Miles? I thought. *I'd like to be his wife.*

Ever since then, I've kind of been a lost cause. And nobody — *not even Jade* — knows how I feel about the boy I will probably never have.

The weird thing is, even though Miles and Jade have no clue about my crush, the two of them have been acting noticeably bizarre toward me this year. Little silences, little looks. Did they figure out my secret? Was it something else? It was making me paranoid, and I was hoping that this summer would be our chance to clear things up.

Miles

I'm not like Jade.

What I mean to say is: I was never burning to get out of Seashell Point. I used to love it here — the salt staining your skin, the crest of the waves, the way everyone kind of lived lazily, sipping cold drinks and discussing which board shorts were best. But my hometown has lost some of its old appeal. My change of heart doesn't have much to do with the impending boardwalk doom written up in today's paper, or what Megan knew about it, or even how Megan's mom mentioned what happened to me.

Everything has to do with me alone — specifically — with what happened last summer.

Ah, yes. That would be my "accident," as my parents like to call it, or my "recovery," as the doctors like to call it, or my "stupidity," as I like to call it.

See, one morning, when I went out to surf —

Screw it; lame intro. Let's be exact. It's not like I can pretend not to know the precise date and time. It wasn't "one morning."

When you're traumatized, you remember everything about what happened up to the very instant: the weather conditions (cloudy, cool, and rough water, i.e., an approaching storm); what you were wearing (Nike wet suit, Expedition waterproof watch, the leather ankle bracelet Jade's father gave you); the other two surfers in the water at the time (Mr. Browning, your old third-grade teacher, and some random tattooed tourist chick you'd seen a few times); the trio of seagulls gliding overhead — like some evil omen — as you strapped the board to your ankle and started paddling out to sea.

Details, details. So, on August 12, at 6:46 A.M., I was floating on my board, flat on my stomach. There I lay, poised to take a particularly choice approaching wave, when I spotted Megan and her mom, standing alone on the boardwalk, watching me.

I shouldn't have thought anything of it. But Megan has issues with her mom. Just like Jade has issues with her dad and sister . . . just like I have issues with both my parents. I thought: *Megan looks bummed. I should do a goofy trick to distract her.*

I remember, too, thinking about the soundtrack to *Dogtown and Z-Boys* — a documentary about these whacked-out group of surfers-turned-skateboarders from Southern California. (Megan forced me to rent it; she's obsessed with weird movies.) And all this was swirling through my head as I turned back to the wave —

It was close, about to break.

I should have back-paddled over it. I should have let it pass.

I should have . . . I should have . . .

See: Surfers, contrary to popular belief, are not "slackers." In fact, the best are very meticulous about how they approach their passion of riding waves. The best are as meticulous as, say, a great lawyer is about practicing the law. (Can we sue the surfboard company for Miles's accident? Answer = "No, they are not liable, but nice try.") Or they are as meticulous as a great doctor is about practicing medicine. ("Miles, with rigorous meds and therapy, your leg will heal in nine months.") You don't think of great doctors and lawyers as slackers. A dozen different smart decisions have to be made quickly, depending on what's coming at you.

I am not a great surfer is what I'm getting at.

I made a dumb decision. I took the wave, thinking I could clear the top of it as it crested — and actually get airborne — then use gravity to propel me down the tube as it curled over me. The problem was the wave was cresting already. My heart was pounding and I was perched on my board, shooting upward at too high an angle . . . and the very, very last thing I remember, before lying on the beach in agony, coughing up seawater, was a glimpse of Megan — staring in horror as the wave swallowed me up and hurled me down to the ocean floor . . .

Whatever.

Enough about all that.

At least I was off my crutches now. I still had a limp. And my left leg continued to ache after six months in a cast and two hours of physical therapy a day. *Woo-hoo!*

But time to look ahead. School was out in three weeks,

today was the first day of the season, it was a beautiful morning, and Megan and Jade were waiting for me. I tried to avoid peering at the surfers as I limped down the boardwalk. Funny: My surf buddies always used to rag on me for being a "girl's best friend." It had always pissed me off. Not anymore. None of *them* had ever visited me in the hospital, except Mr. Browning.

"So, Miles, are you ready to party, or what?" Jade said by way of hello.

Party? "You're not on drugs, are you?" I asked.

"Ha! I just asked Meg that exact same thing!" She smiled behind her bug-eyed shades. "Great minds think alike. But actually the last thing I want to do this summer is *think*. No thinking at all."

"No thinking, huh?" I shot an anxious glance at Megan. "Great plan, Jade."

Megan shrugged.

"So . . . what's with the fancy dress?" I asked Megan. "*Is* there a party?"

"My mom had an interview early this morning, and she made me tag along." She shook her head, her cheeks pink. "You read the *Register*, right?"

I nodded glumly. "Yeah. I don't believe it."

"Don't believe what?" Jade asked.

Megan chewed her lip, afraid to answer.

I could relate. Saying something out loud makes it a lot more real. (Try saying: "I broke my leg in three places," and mean it.)

29

"Some real-estate big shot is coming to town," I explained in the silence. "The rumor is he wants to tear down the boardwalk to make room for something else, something bigger and different. Nobody knows what, though. Or at least nobody claims to know anything." I turned back to Megan.

"If my mom knows anything, she's not telling me," Megan muttered.

Jade sighed and arched an eyebrow. "Oh, come on, you guys. That's just gossip. Meg, your mom said the same thing about the petting zoo a few years ago, when those penguins escaped. You honestly think this town would let somebody tear down the boardwalk? Nothing's gonna happen. And even if it does, we don't need this crummy boardwalk anymore, because now we have a new place to meet — and for once it belongs totally to us: the Jade Cohen party house."

My eyes narrowed. I was used to Jade's high-speed and nonsensical monologues, but this one was more deranged than most. "The Jade Cohen . . . what?"

"My dad's leaving the house to Turkey and me this summer," she said, rubbing her hands together mischievously.

"Are you serious? That's so cool!"

Jade laughed. "Well, yeah, it will be, because I'm planning on locking Turkey in the closet with her law books and feeding her scraps, so she doesn't bother us —"

"Oh, my God, you guys!" Megan grabbed each of our arms and yanked us close together. "That's him. That's Arnold Roth, the real-estate guy." She jerked her head toward the beach.

"And look at him. He's already plotting major destruction. I'm serious. Look at him!"

"Where?" Jade and I whispered at the same time.

I followed Megan's gaze over the railing to a secluded spot of sand, maybe thirty yards from where the first sunbathers were starting to crack open their cheesy beach reads. There I spotted a guy who looked sort of like George Clooney, but fatter. He stood barefoot, squinting at the boardwalk's support pylons, in a white sun hat, blue button-down long-sleeved shirt, and rolled-up seersucker pants. (A definite tourist.)

It did seem as if he were plotting something. He barely even moved.

A blonde girl stood next to him. A natural blonde, too. Living in a resort town your whole life as a natural blond, you develop a sixth sense for these things. She faced the opposite direction, toward the ocean, her long curls flapping in the wind. She was also barefoot, in a backless shirt and cutoffs. Judging by her flawless skin and length of her slender legs, she was probably as tall as I am and not much older.

"Who's that with him?" I asked. "Trophy wife?"

Neither Megan nor Jade replied.

"Why, do you think she's hot?" Jade asked, laughing.

"I . . . well . . . I mean, I can't see her face, but . . ." I left it at that.

Megan pursed her lips. "That's his daughter, Lily-Ann,"

she said. "She's going to Williams in the fall." Something about her tone seemed to add: *She's also a huge spoiled tourist who thinks she's God's gift to planet Earth.*

"So I guess that means she's not invited to the Jade Cohen party house, huh?" I joked, trying to lighten the mood.

Jade glared up at me over the tops of her sunglasses. "Miles, so far we only have three partygoers. Two of us are girls. If you're going to invite somebody, it has to be a guy to even the ratio. That's rule number one. Girls cannot outnumber guys under any circumstances. The playing field must be level at all times. After all, we all want to get lucky this summer, don't we?"

I should have made a wisecrack right then.

I should have shot back with something like *"Fine, I choose Brian Ashe and I'll raise you Sean Edwards. Now if you'll excuse me, I'm going to scope out this Lily-Ann girl."*

I should have . . . I should have . . .

I would have, too — if it were a year ago. If it were last summer, before the accident, Jade and I would be ragging on each other by now. But our relationship hadn't been the same since September. And it wasn't because I couldn't surf.

For the first time in our lives, we had a secret between us that Megan didn't know.

So most of all, right then, I should have acted natural for Megan's sake.

"You guys?" Megan said.

Suddenly, I noticed Megan's gaze darting between us.

"Yeah?" I asked.

"I'm really not sure about this party house thing," she said quietly.

"What, are you kidding?" Jade asked, laughing. "It was your idea, Meg."

"Yeah, but . . . Okay: We have your house to ourselves this summer. But think about it, guys. Jade . . . it was just like you said — this is our last summer before senior year, maybe even the last summer we'll really get a chance to hang out and have fun together, just the three of us. Yeah, we should definitely have barbecues and stuff, and parties, and even invite some tourists if we want, but . . ."

I cocked my head at her. That little outburst probably represented the most words Megan had ever uttered continuously in her life.

"So, you're saying . . . ?" Jade asked, pushing her sunglasses back up her nose.

"I'm saying the three of us should make a pact," Megan stated.

Now I felt as if I'd been beamed into some bizarre alternate universe. The last time Megan took a proactive stance about anything was when she decided to keep cleaning houses for a summer job after Jade got fired for being naughty on the job. She'd kissed a tourist's son . . . whatever. But right after that, both Jade and I had tried to coax Megan into working at a concession stand on the boardwalk. Her response? She'd said it would be "too distracting" to work near Jade and me. We *still* haven't stopped calling her on how lame that decision was.

But a pact . . . this was unexplored territory.

"Go on," Jade prodded.

"The three of us should hang out as much as we can this summer. Hooking up with random tourist people will be too —"

"Distracting?" Jade and I both said at the same time. We grinned at each other, almost as a reflex. Panic crept up in me. We turned back to Megan.

"Exactly," she said.

I held my breath. My pulse picked up a notch. I waited for Jade to speak.

"Well, I'm in," she said briskly, extending a hand to Megan. "I think it's a brilliant idea. No kissing tourists. We'll discipline ourselves, have a ball — *and* bond."

Megan heaved a huge sigh of relief. "Really?" she asked.

I sighed, too, and I wasn't even sure why.

"Absolutely," Jade said, raising her right hand. "Daughter-of-a-hippie's honor. We don't break our word. Now let's get to school, shall we, party people?"

Megan turned to me. I forced a fake smile as I shook her hand, watching Jade stroll down the boardwalk toward Main Street.

I'd never faked a smile with Megan before. It made me feel gross, like how my parents fake smiles with people they despise — but I guess I'd been faking a lot of things with her all year. Keeping a secret from one of your best friends is just another term for faking, isn't it?

But the worst part? I wasn't even thinking about Megan's feelings. I was thinking of all the possible things that could go wrong with this pact, of all the right decisions I could make if I were good at anything (as in: *Tell Megan what happened with Jade*) . . . and mostly how if anything *did* go wrong with the pact, I might lose my friends.

I dropped Megan's hand.

She stepped closer, with a puzzled grin. "You okay?"

I shrugged.

Funny: Worrying about Megan had turned me *into* Megan. Well, the guy version, anyway, the (not so) strong silent type.

Maybe Jade was right. Maybe "no thinking" should be the rally cry of the summer. I never used to think so much, except about how cool it would be to win a surfing competition, or hook up with the perfect girl, or turn into a giraffe and hang out all day at Pete's Petting Zoo.

I'm not that guy anymore.

Part Two
The Tourist Girl

Jade

So: the big secret.

Before I confess, I want to share my thoughts on secrets in general. Like babies, once they're born, secrets lie around and fatten up. At first, there isn't much to worry about. You tend to them and you put them down for sleepy time. They're a presence, though. They're never *not* there. Then they start to think for themselves . . . and pretty soon they wander off on their own, and that's when they get a lot more complicated and worrisome.

Okay, and one more thing: (I know I'm stalling.)

I dare *anyone* to swear that they haven't considered hooking up with a friend — that is to say, a friend who is an attractive member of the opposite sex. At least once. Even if it's just a fleeting notion. Even if it's a boy or girl you've known your whole life, who may be your *best* friend, you wonder: What might their lips taste like? Would they put their hands in my hair? Are we secretly in love?

Isn't that what love is supposed to be? A lifetime of hooking up with your best friend, who also happens to be an attractive member of the opposite sex?

Just throwing it out there.

*   *   *

Here's what happened.

On the morning of August 12 last year, I emerged from a hot shower, post cold ocean dip. My cell phone rang. I was wrapped in my bathrobe about to dry my hair. It wasn't even seven o'clock. I marched into my bedroom and frowned at the caller ID.

Meg? Now? I remember being annoyed. I remember thinking that she probably wanted me to poach some cleaning supplies from Dad because she'd run out of Windex and couldn't make it to the store on time — before she had to clean Glenn Close's house or some other such tourist nonsense. *You should have worked on the boardwalk with Miles and me*, I remember wanting to tell her.

"What's up, Meg?" I answered flatly. "Top o' the morning to ya."

I didn't hear anything but sobbing.

After two sleepless nights, the hysterics, the disbelief, the denial — and finally the call from Eloise Gordon, Miles's mom, *"He's going to be okay!"* — we got the news that it was safe to visit him in the hospital. If you've never been to an ICU, intensive care unit, I don't recommend a sightseeing trip. The bright lights, the beeping, the gurneys, the IV's . . . everything bathed in a blinding white, white, white: the floors, the scrubs, the surgical masks — *I* felt sick. And then we saw him.

His eyes were closed. He was hooked up to about a dozen different tubes and wires. A nurse hovered over him. They'd shaved his long blond hair. He had a bruise on his forehead. His legs were elevated. The left leg was wrapped in a cast. His tan looked fake, almost orange. It was almost as if you could see how pale he would have been if he hadn't spent the summer in the sun. He didn't look like Miles.

"Miles?" his mom whispered. She kneaded his shoulder. The nurse didn't seem to like that, but she didn't say anything. "Sweetie? Megan and Jade came to visit."

His eyelids fluttered. His pupils were little pinpricks; there was only brown. He smiled at Megan. He didn't notice I was there.

"Thank God, you're here," he croaked.

I tried to say hello, but my throat was too parched. I began tugging at my hair.

"He's heavily sedated," the nurse said.

"You saved my . . . my . . . life, Megan." He closed his eyes again.

"Actually, Mr. Browning saved your life," Megan whispered. "And that other surfer, Bruce Willis's personal assistant. What's her name? I've been in such a fog since this whole thing." She glanced up at me. "Jade?"

I didn't answer. (How could I? I couldn't even speak.) Instead I bolted.

As I ran down those horrible white halls, I thought: *How would I know what Bruce Willis's assistant's name is? You're the one with the mom on the tourist board.*

*   *   *

Now flash forward to the morning of September 14.

Miles came home, via wheelchair. I ditched school with permission to welcome him back. To be fair, Mr. Browning intervened on my behalf. (*"You think this poor kid wants to spend all day alone?"*) But Megan didn't ditch. She didn't have to. She'd been taking the bus from Seashell Point to the county hospital three times a week to visit him. She'd been the loyal friend. She'd sat by his bed, listened to him — all of it. She'd been completely sympathetic about my *not* having visited Miles since that first day.

"I understand," she kept saying.

Even worse, she meant it. Megan never says anything unless she means it. She barely talks at all, so her words count. But what was there to understand? That I ran out on him like a coward? That I was jealous of how Miles honed in on her instead of me in his drugged-out stupor? That I was too fragile to go to an ICU? That I wasn't as good a person as Megan was?

I'd arranged everything with Mr. and Mrs. Gordon earlier.

They would drop him off; I would fix him lunch and put him to bed while they went to work — and so on and so forth. And of course, I'd help him catch up on the missed schoolwork and gossip for a few hours. Then they'd be back to relieve me for Miles-care in the early afternoon. Essentially, it was a babysitting gig. But I had an angle. In all her visits, Megan had only brought Miles flowers as a gift.

"Flowers." "Miles."

Say those two words together. It's like saying: *"Turquoise." "Jade."*

They don't match.

I'm sure he appreciated the gesture, but flowers were empty, an allergenic Hallmark card. Megan could have done better. So I bought him a skateboard.

It cost me my entire summer earnings from working at Amusement Alley, plus a couple of bucks that Dad gave me. And yes, I know, it might have seemed a little cruel at first. But I knew that Miles would get the joke. (Especially since I'd pre-tagged the board with several kiddie stickers of giraffes.) Miles had always maintained a sort of reverse-snobbery against skateboarding — even though as far as I could tell, surfing and skateboarding is pretty much the same thing. One's the water version; one's the land version. Right? But out loud, Miles always said, "Skating is for the tourists who rip down the boardwalk like they own it."

When his mom wheeled him in that morning, I couldn't quite breathe. The door opened, and the sunshine poured into the front hall. I mean, I could breathe but my heart was thumping a little too hard for breathing to be pleasant.

Then I saw him.

He was himself.

The spark was back in his eyes, and his hair had grown

enough so that it had a sort of mid-career Brad Pitt thing going. Honestly, I didn't even notice the cast. He smiled, and then his mouth fell open.

"A skateboard?" he said, laughing.

I tried to smile back. My throat tightened. My eyes began to sting.

"Listen, Jade, honey, I really have to run to work," Mrs. Gordon mumbled, locking the wheelchair brakes. She patted down her pockets and handbag, checking for essential belongings — keys, wallet, phone. "I know you have a funny sense of humor, but don't let Miles ride that thing. Thanks so much, dear —"

With that, she slammed the door behind her.

Miles's eyes moistened.

"Hi," he said.

"Hi," I said.

"What's up?"

"I brought you a present."

"I thought you were scared," he said.

"Of what?"

"Of seeing me."

I tried to swallow again, but it hurt. "Do you like it?" I choked out. My voice was hoarse, like a criminal in a mob movie.

"Do I like what?"

"The skateboard."

"I love it." He lifted a hand, reaching out toward me. "Can I see it?"

"Sure."

I marched forward and placed the skateboard in his lap, all the while thinking: *Whatever you do, Jade, don't cry.*

He tossed the skateboard on the floor. It landed with a rubbery thud, and then rolled toward the hallway.

"What?" I cried. "You don't like it, do you?"

"I like it a lot. I just like more that you — I just like that you're here."

"Wouldn't miss it," I croaked.

He held out his arms to bring me in for a hug.

I sat on his lap and hugged him back for a long time. He smelled clean and new like fabric softener. Miles used to smell like the beach.

We pulled apart. We looked at each other. Everything seemed to be a blur.

He kissed me. On the lips. I kissed him back.

I ran my fingers through his hair. His shoulders were just as strong and firm as they'd been before the accident. I'd massaged them on lots of occasions, for fun, even to tease him after he'd surfed. But now was different. We pressed close together, and our kiss deepened, as if the harder we kissed, the less real Miles's accident would seem. Nothing made sense. Our tongues touched. *This is Miles*, I kept thinking. *Miles. He's like your brother.*

But the kissing went on. Soon, I felt his fingers running over *my* shoulders, through *my* hair. We both sighed a little, into each other's mouth. We kissed like that for a long, long time.

His lips were softer than I'd thought they would be.

Afterward I left the room and washed my face and made him lunch: microwave fried clams. He laughed.

Then he sat in bed while we played a round of poker. Right, and a final crucial detail —

We never talked about the make-out session again. Ever.

Megan

When you clean mansions for a summer job, you're invisible. You're not supposed to speak unless spoken to. You just scrub the thousand-dollar furniture and launder the Prada clothes, and keep silent. It's a requirement. That's a big plus for me, right there. It's probably the reason I'd decided to stay on, doing Jade's job, cleaning up for tourists instead of working on the boardwalk. Mom has also asked me a million times to "help out" every single summer at the tourist board. To "help out" is a euphemism for answering outrageous phone calls and e-mails. *"Hi! You want to parasail with J-Lo for your birthday? Great! Eighty grand!"*

The second plus of cleaning our town's mansions, of course, are all the loony conversations you might overhear. I may be shy, but in the words of *The Seashell Register*, I do rejoice in a good scandal.

To give you some examples — and these are real quotes (the names haven't been changed, in order to incriminate the guilty):

- "Darling, please. I know all about you and the child psychologist. When you come home smelling like our daughter's Magic Markers, I know where you've been. I really *am* a househusband — except at the beach."

47

- "If you were so worried about your body, Madeline, you wouldn't lie about that Cohen idiot with the gray ponytail. Does yoga include a good banging?"
- "I must have passed out with her, Theodore. We'd been drinking chardonnay in the sun all afternoon. But no, I am not a lesbian."

And, as bad as eavesdropping is, I've learned a lot from it. In fact, I would say that more than 90 percent of the tourists are actually pretty cool. They're just going through the normal family stuff . . . only in a different tax bracket.

Then I met Lily-Ann Roth.

School was over. Jade's dad had left for San Francisco, and the party planning had begun. Turquoise was locked away all day in her dad's bedroom, poring over obscure law journals.

Jade and Miles were back at their usual jobs: Jade at the Jupiter Bounce for toddlers in Amusement Alley and Miles three stands down at Sonny's Clam Shack.

Things were good.

The Roth's mansion is *the* prime Seashell Point spot for tourists. It's smaller than some of the others farther down the beach, but it's the most luxurious and it's got "location, location, location," as in, it's right next to the boardwalk. There's a garden, too — a garden on the beach, encased in a huge, climate-controlled greenhouse. I'm not kidding. You can water your roses and stare out at the ocean. It is entirely ludicrous, but somehow wonderful.

Every bedroom has a flat-screen TV, a king-size bed, Wi-Fi, and a bathroom with a Jacuzzi. There are three Roths: Arnold, Cheryl, and Lily-Ann. That leaves three empty bedrooms — three bedrooms that don't need to be cleaned — a perfect gig for a cleaning person: half the job, all the fun. In theory, things were about as sweet as they could get. But when I showed up at the Roths' on my first official working day . . . Who answered the door?

Mom.

"What are *you* doing here?" I asked.

"Megan! I — I suppose we could have walked here together. I was just talking with Mr. Roth," she said in a strange, high-pitched voice.

I hoped to God that they were not having an affair.

Before she could go on, Lily-Ann swept into view.

Lily-Ann looked about as sour as my mood. She gave me a quick once-over, then dug her iPhone out of her skirt and began texting someone. Her flat stomach and belly button were plainly visible under her too-small spaghetti-strap top. I have to say, though, if she had a soul (I'd assumed she didn't), she would have been pretty. She had great tanned skin, like Jade's, a freckled button nose, and intense blue eyes. I could see why Miles had thought she was a trophy wife. I was also trying very hard to forget about that.

"Megan," Mom began, "this is Lily-Ann —"

"I know, Mom. You introduced us in your office last summer."

Lily-Ann's lips were too red and narrow, like a pair of little worms. They didn't smile or scowl; they *slithered*.

Mom laughed a little too loudly. "Oh, that's right! Anyway, I thought it would be nice if you could show her around town while Mr. Roth and I discussed some business."

Then Mr. Roth appeared by his daughter's side. His belly poked out from under his shirt, too. Only his stomach wasn't flat. The shirt looked like he'd won it at a game stand on the boardwalk — it was stained with soda and read OVER FORTY AND FEELING FOXY. I prayed he'd just been exercising. No grown man would greet a stranger at his own front door if he were sweating, unkempt, and wearing bike shorts. Well, unless the stranger in question was the invisible house cleaner.

"Megan Kim!" he shouted jovially.

"Hello, Mr. Roth. How are —"

"You've lived here your whole life, Megan," he interrupted. "I figured Lily-Ann could benefit from a tour guide. Besides, there's nothing here to clean. We just moved in two weeks ago. We haven't had a chance to make a mess yet! *Hauggh . . .*"

When he laughed, he ended up coughing.

Is my mom is having an affair with the guy who wants to tear down the boardwalk? But, no. She'd tell me about something *that* huge. Plus, people don't laugh when they're having an affair. They act snippy. That's why Mom had always laughed, a decade ago, when Jade and I kept trying to set up her and Jade's father — because it never worked out. In our defense, why wouldn't we try to set them up? The way Jade and I saw it, we'd be sisters and we'd both have a mom and dad. There's five-year-old logic for you. So this really must have been about business. But that wasn't a mood lifter, either. In a way, it was just as bad. Mom was in on the boardwalk plan, whatever it was.

"So whaddaya say, kids?" Mr. Roth said, ushering Lily-Ann toward the door. She kept texting, but didn't protest. "Meg? Feel like being a tour guide?"

"Megan," I corrected without thinking.

Mom glowered at me.

I forced a pained smile. "Sorry . . . it's just — only certain people call me Meg."

"Well, I like Meg!" Mr. Roth answered. "So, add one more person to the list."

As I stood in the doorway, I imagined what it would feel like to grab Lily-Ann's iPhone and cram it down Mr. Roth's throat.

Lily-Ann finally looked up at me. She slipped her iPhone back into her skirt. She cast a long gaze at her father.

"Thanks for showing me around, *Megan*," she said, emphasizing my name. "It is Megan, isn't it?"

I grinned, for real this time. I think she might have smiled at me, too.

Those wormy red lips were tough to read.

Jade

Miles's and my first fight of the summer should be another Seashell Point tradition. It should be like the first tourist scandal (yet to happen), "Clam-Fest" (don't ask), the Fourth of July fireworks. Every year, right about the same time, Miles and I get into a fight about something stupid.

Chalk it up to boredom. I sell tickets at the Jupiter Bounce. Yes, because I was fired from my first summer job ever. Yes, because I was caught making out with a tourist named Derek Madison on his rent-a-mansion couch while Megan was upstairs polishing the master bedroom mirrors. In my defense: Derek was truly tall, dark, and handsome; he played guitar; he claimed that he *wrote a song for [me]. It's called 'Cleaning Lady.'"*

Yes, he didn't have much of a brain, but who needs one in Seashell Point? Luckily (or not) his family left town forever after they walked in on us in full-on French-kiss mode, the guitar long forgotten beside us. His parents were too outraged at the scandal to return. But, in fairness, our town's scandal is best witnessed from a safe distance . . . another reason I want to be whisked away by a gorgeous rock star. (Derek, sweetie, it won't be you. When you get a day job, please do <u>NOT</u> quit.)

Anyway, my boss, Sarah — a portly fiend of indeterminate age with an even worse sense of style than Dad — insists I arrive promptly at nine every morning, "just in case."

No child has ever arrived before two in the afternoon.

Two P.M. is when local day care ends. Either that or the au pairs are too exhausted to spoil their kids any longer. Honestly, I don't even know. All I know is that's when the business begins. Pack 'em in for five minutes at a time, let 'em shriek and jump and push one another and do backflips and occasionally knock heads or elbows and cry. (Nobody ever *really* gets hurt; I can actually be a very strict monitor if I see a bully.) Ah, the joys of summer employment.

Likewise, Miles's boss, Donny, insists that Miles arrive at nine A.M., as well — even though no sane person would buy fried clams before noon. Well, except for Donny. Consider that Donny accidentally named his clam shack "Sonny's" instead of "Donny's." In his defense, the S key and the D key are right next to each other on the computer keyboard. (Although the signs are all hand-painted.) But anybody could make that mistake. And Sonny's has a nicer ring to it, too.

All this is a long way of saying that for the past two summers, Miles and I have had about three hours every morning with nothing to do. We pick that same strategic spot on the railing — the very first spot that Miles chose back in the day — where we can both monitor the clam shack and the Jupiter Bounce, "just in case" . . . and we BS. We rag on tourists ("Where did Sean Edwards get that cheesy seashell necklace? And why is he even back this summer?") and, of course, we rag on each other ("Miles, that knapsack is grotesque. Is it *camouflage?*").

But inevitably, the ragging turns from lighthearted to sour . . . like curdled milk.

Maybe this time, our secret fed into the fight. I don't know.

It started stupidly and innocently enough, as all our fights do.

Miles asked, "So Turquoise is cool with the whole pact party?" That was what we'd started calling it.

"I don't know. I swear; I've seen her only four times since she's been home. She stays up all night studying and is asleep when I'm gone in the morning. We don't eat together, ever. She's mostly like this disembodied voice, shouting from behind some closed door. 'Jade, turn the TV down!' 'Jade, do the dishes for once. I'll empty!' 'Jade, you left the screen door open!' Great to have Turkey home again."

Miles laughed.

"What?"

He drummed his fingers on the boardwalk railing, Megan-style, watching the passersby. He shook his head. "Nothing," he said.

"You know I hate the word *nothing*. If you ever use it again, I'll take back —" I cut myself off. I was about to say: *I'll take back that skateboard.*

In the past three weeks, his limp had all but disappeared. He'd actually tried the board out a couple of times up and down the boardwalk . . . nothing fancy, just getting his balance back. His first try, I nearly cried. (I ran to the bathroom, stammering that he'd undercooked the day's batch of fried clams.) He kept it in his knapsack most of the time, though, except to look at it.

"You'll take back what?" he asked.

"Every nice thing I've ever said about you," I replied.

"Name one nice thing you've said about me," he joked.

"Ha! Didn't I say you had nice hair once? You have nice hair. You're the only natural blond in Seashell Point. That's something."

"Not the only one. Lily-Ann Roth."

I rolled my eyes. "Why are we talking about some snooty tourist we don't even know? I thought we were talking about my sister. You were going to say something about her." I snatched my sunglasses out of my bag and put them on. *Note to self: Use the Jupiter Bounce earnings to invest in a pricier pair of shades than the $15.99 special at Clement's. Shades that will rival Lily-Ann Roth's.* "Talk Turkey, Miles."

He drew in a deep breath. "All I was going to say was . . . maybe she wants to be invited to the pact party."

I stared at him through the dark lenses. "I'm sorry?"

Miles shrugged. "I just thought it might be, I dunno, rude or some crap to have this rager right in the house while she's upstairs. I just don't know if you always think things through, Jade —"

Fury rose in me. *You mean the way you should have thought before you kissed me?*

"Forget it," I snapped. "Turquoise doesn't *do* parties. If

55

anything, she'd want to police it and chaperone. She was forty years old when she was born, and nothing will change that, Miles."

Miles's eyes darkened.

"You're so stubborn."

"My house, my rules."

I bit my lip. Okay, that was unfair. I felt a twinge of guilt — and I was almost about to apologize, when Miles's face suddenly brightened.

"What?"

He nodded down the boardwalk, toward the south side. "Speak of the devil."

"Turkey?" I whirled around . . . and froze.

It wasn't my sister. It was Megan and Lily-Ann Roth.

Walking side by side. Chatting. Smiling.

Megan waved.

My mouth hung open.

Megan never *talked* to the tourists.

But . . .

"Hey, guys," she said. She threw her arm around the new girl's shoulder. "I want you to meet my friend, Lily-Ann."

Megan

Neither Miles nor Jade said anything at first. I couldn't blame them. If Jade had walked up and pulled the same stunt with me, I would have been speechless, too. Obviously. I would have never seen it coming.

But the very first words out of Lily-Ann's mouth, in the ten minutes it took for us to walk from her mansion to Amusement Alley, were: "You know what would piss my dad off more than anything? Being best friends with the hired help who cleans up after me."

I didn't answer.

"I'm sorry, that was really rude," she said.

"No worries."

"Really?"

"I've heard worse. You should have heard what Mr. Madison said two years ago when he fired Jade. . . . Never mind." I shook my head, keeping my eyes on the planks as we plodded up the boardwalk steps from the beach. "But, uh, if that's the case, why did he ask me to show you around town? He expects me to be friendly, right?"

She snorted in a way that reminded me of Jade. "He just wanted to get rid of us so he could talk to your mom about his big plans for your town. Whenever he laughs a lot, it means he's not really there. His mind is on a hundred different things. And he was exercising before, so the endorphins were flowing. He was in an altered state."

Jeez. I could barely understand her. "What *are* his big plans?" I asked.

"I'd tell you if I knew," she said with a sigh, flinging her blonde hair over one shoulder. "But the last thing I want to do is find out about his business. Sometimes, ignorance really *is* bliss." She waved her hand at the long, weathered expanse of wood ahead of us — still relatively deserted at this hour, just some toddlers in strollers and young moms, and seagulls cawing and circling overhead. The salty wind was light enough so we could hear the creaking under our flip-flops. Hers were bejeweled, naturally. "I do know that he wants to tear this thing down and put something else in its place. What, I don't know. He's mostly built hotels, so I bet it's something like that."

My stomach squeezed. Jade was wrong; it *wasn't* gossip. It was real.

I tried to imagine what the beach would look like without the boardwalk. It would look like Boca Raton, where Jade's grandma lived. In other words: cheesy, bland, modern. Different. I tried to shake the thought from my mind. Once the boardwalk was gone, Miles and Jade wouldn't be able to meet me at the same spot, and nobody would be able to notice a surfer in trouble — except from a hotel room balcony.

"So, you're going to Williams in the fall, huh?" I asked. "That's awesome."

"I'm glad somebody thinks so." She snorted again.

I glanced at her out of the corner of my eye. "What do you mean?"

"My dad thinks I should have gone to Harvard. He went to Harvard. Unfortunately, I didn't get into Harvard. So I'm not going to Harvard." Each time she said *Harvard*, she pronounced it with just a little more venom. "My mother's generous contribution to Williams seems to have had a much bigger impact than my dad's lack of contributions to his alma mater. So I'm going to Williams."

"Well, maybe Williams will be more fun?" I offered lamely.

"What would be more fun is not going to college at all."

I laughed. "You really think so?"

"No, not really." She sighed again, sounding about twice her age.

I stole another quick peek at her. She was smiling curiously at all the cheap concession stands, as if she'd never seen one in her life. All were closed. On the south side, it's strictly swimwear and surf gear, so none of the owners show up before eleven at the earliest. Most look like washed-up eighties Hair Band members. Some actually are. That's where the brilliantly unoriginal stand names like "Surf's Up, Bro!" or "Hang Ten for Under Fifty Clams!" come from. I almost felt embarrassed. There was a very good chance Lily-Ann *hadn't* seen a cheap concession stand in her life, particularly if she'd vacationed in places like St. Maarten before coming to rustic old Seashell Point. She'd probably feel a lot more comfortable downtown. Come to think of it, downtown essentially was

St. Maarten, only dressed up eighteenth-century-Mid-Atlantic-coastal style.

"Where are *you* applying, Megan?" she asked.

"I was thinking about NYU," I answered absently. "I researched on-line, and they have these great internship programs where you can work in the city government with people who try to solve local problems —" I coughed. "Sorry. As if you care."

"No, I do." She paused for a second and turned toward me, fixing me with an intense stare. "It's just . . ." Her wormy lips formed what looked like an actual smile. "Okay, I don't really. But I do think it's cool. I mean all I care about is pissing off my dad. You know what he always tells me? 'You can do better.' It's like this weird mantra. Better than what?"

I lifted my shoulders. I'd just met her. Besides, I *was* the hired help. I couldn't answer that question. It wasn't part of the job description. I should have been Soft-Scrubbing their marble tub.

"The first time he ever said that to me was when I started going out with this guy who got kicked out of my old school," she went on. "Roland Evans. His dad is some big-time Manhattan shrink, so of course the kid is crazy. He was hot though, in a kind of bad-boy way, and funny as hell — he just didn't give a crap about anything. He used to skip classes and troll the school halls singing '*RO-Land, RO-Land, RO-Land . . .*' You know, like that rap song, '*Rollin', rollin', rollin' . . .*' and this one time he started singing it when we were in the janitor's closet, and I was —"

"How . . . how about I show you downtown?" I stammered before she could finish. My cheeks were hot. Jade and I hardly ever talked about sex. Especially hot sex in a janitor's closet. Neither of us had gotten there yet. Not even close. "I mean, there really isn't much to see on the boardwalk right now."

She brushed a long blonde curl out of her face and gave me another apologetic half smile. "I'm making you uncomfortable, aren't I?"

"No," I lied.

"Hey, here's in idea. Why don't you show me the spots where all the cute guys hang out? I haven't really seen too many so far."

My gaze wandered toward the north end of the boardwalk. I shielded the sun from my face, standing on my tiptoes — and sure enough, spotted Jade and Miles leaning against the railing, maybe a quarter mile away. Miles's tousled blond hair was impossible to mistake. And, of course, Jade was waving her hands dramatically. Their first summer fight. Duh.

I didn't want Lily-Ann to see Miles.

"There is this one guy you should meet . . ."

"Sean Edwards?" she asked.

My hand dropped. I turned to her. I wasn't sure whether to laugh. "You know Sean Edwards?"

"Yeah. I met him yesterday. He's taking care of our greenhouse this summer."

I forgot myself for a second. "He *is*?" My eyebrows twisted in a knot.

"Why, is that a problem?" she asked.

Yes! I answered silently. *And more than one!* Indeed, many problems. The first? I'd be spending the summer working with a doofus I'd been stupid enough to kiss a few times in the past. (Thank God he'd be confined to the greenhouse.) But I wasn't even really thinking about that. I was thinking: *Sean Edwards is a tourist. Why did he get a summer job tending to another tourist's garden? Tourists don't work. This is a first in the history of Seashell Point. This is wrong!*

Lily-Ann smirked.

And after a long look at her, it hit me.

"Oh," I said out loud. I had to laugh. Sean must have Googled the Roth family — or maybe he even knew them. He did live in D.C. most of the year but wealthy families hung out with other wealthy families. Yup. One glimpse of Lily-Ann at some society ball . . . well, the thought of tending to her garden was too good to pass up. Classic horn dog. I had to hand it to the guy. Maybe he was cleverer than I thought.

"Oh, what?" she asked.

"Oh, well," I said. "I'm not sure of his gardening skills, but he's okay."

She drew closer. "You know him?"

I knew my face was bright red. I began to perspire. "I made out with him once," I blurted in as hushed a voice as possible.

"You *did*?" She grabbed my arm and giggled. "Oh, my God."

"What?" I asked nervously. "You just said he was cute."

"Yeah, but you're way hotter than he is cute."

"Excuse me?"

62

Lily-Ann's eyes twinkled. "You can do better, Megan Kim. You can do better."

I laughed again. "Well ... I ... that's ... I don't know. Nice of you to say?"

"I wouldn't say it if I didn't mean it," she replied. "Look, what do you think would piss off my dad the most? Hooking up with the semi-cute gardener, *and* being best friends with my hot house cleaner, right? Which, judging by how cool you've treated me so far, seems in my best interest in terms of this town. Imagine it: my boy-toy and my new BFF in the same house for a whole summer."

"Please tell me you're kidding," I muttered.

"Of course. No. Yes. A combination."

My God. This girl truly *was* insane. But in kind of a good way. She certainly wasn't like any of the other self-obsessed, phony tourists I've known. Plus, now that I thought about it, she was straightforward — very different from Miles and Jade, at least lately. Those two had been acting beyond weird for the past year, and I knew they thought I didn't notice.

My mood swelled, and I couldn't help but think somewhere deep inside: *If I play Lily-Ann's BFF and Sean plays her boy-toy, there's no chance that Miles will hook up with her.*

And I knew just when to put that plan into action.

"So what do you say?" Lily-Ann asked. "Ready to help your boss out?"

I nodded. "You know, a really good friend of mine is planning a party because she has her house to herself. Do you want to come?"

Miles

At first, I couldn't focus on Lily-Ann Roth. I should have; she was even prettier close-up, but I couldn't stop staring at Megan.

I'd never seen her act so affectionate with anyone. Not even Jade. Of course, Jade wasn't all that affectionate, either. The last time the two of them had hugged in public was at Jade's bat-mitzvah. Plus, Megan was wearing an apron. She must have forgotten to take it off before she'd ventured out.

"Meg, you know you're wearing your apron, right?" Jade asked. "I can still see the spaghetti stains from last summer."

Megan and Lily-Ann looked at each other. Then they giggled. Lily-Ann took Megan by the shoulder; she spun her around, untied her apron — and tossed it into the nearest garbage can. A seagull landed on the railing nearby, studying the apron as if it wanted to hop in after it. *A bird!* I said to myself. *That's what I am right now: a creature with a brain the size of a bird. I have no idea what's going on.* I turned to Jade.

"You're right, Miles," Jade said loudly. She stared at Lily-Ann. "In answer to your unspoken question, we have entered some sort of bizarre alternate universe."

"I'm sorry," Megan murmured. "Miles, Jade . . . I was just telling Lily-Ann about the Jade Cohen party house."

I stepped forward. If everyone else had gone insane, I might as well join the crowd. "Hi, I'm Miles Gordon," I said in a TV-announcer voice. "I'm not only the fry cook at Sonny's Clam Shack, I also receive bribes."

Lily-Ann laughed. It was a musical laugh, not at all forced. She shook my hand, lingering for a while. Her eyes were deep, deep blue, and her fingers were long — a lot like Megan's, actually . . . only they were as tan as Jade's. Her thin lips curled up in a flirtatious smile. "So you're the boy I've been hearing so much about," she said.

I dropped her hand. "What do you mean?" I asked. My voice squeaked.

"The one who takes bribes?" she said drily. She spoke as if we'd been in on an inside joke for years. "From Sonny's Clam Shack?"

"That's me!" I glanced toward the stand. Donny was just arriving. He, too, was wearing an apron — only his was more stained than Megan's, and it wasn't nearly as flattering, seeing as he weighed about five times as much as all of us combined. He hadn't shaved in a while, either. He gave me the finger.

Lily-Ann giggled again. "So that's your boss, huh?"

"Yeah, but his mood improves as we draw closer to nighttime."

"Hey!" Donny shouted. He hiccuped. "Stop showing off your skateboard to the ladies and start frying up some freaking clams!"

"You have a skateboard?" Lily-Ann asked.

Reflexively, I clutched the straps of my knapsack. "I . . . uh . . . well, yeah. But it's in here. It's in my . . . backpack." (*Why does saying the word "backpack" out loud make me sound like a six-year-old? Or does it?*)

Lily-Ann smirked. "Did you choose your backpack yourself? I mean, the color scheme? Camouflage is very —"

"Fox News?" Jade interrupted.

"Rugged?" Megan suggested.

"Hey!" Donny shouted once more. "Show off your skate skills or fry up some freaking clams! That's an executive order!"

I gave *him* the finger.

This practice of giving each other the finger began when Donny visited me in the hospital — as diligently as Megan did, almost every other afternoon. I would wake up in a pain-killer haze and see Donny, grinning and giving me the finger. I had no choice but to return the favor. Especially since he told me that the accident/recovery/stupidity was no excuse for missing work.

"Hey!" Lily-Ann chimed in. "Show off your skate skills."

I had to smile. "Well, now you've asked for it."

Megan and Jade watched me, openmouthed, as I slung my backpack off my shoulder. I heaved out the big, clunky board. I wasn't sure what I was thinking. And actually that's really the whole point . . . I *wasn't* thinking, which was nice for the first time in a long while. All I did (at least consciously) was avoid their eyes. I hopped on and gave myself a little kick start on the wrong foot, to see if Lily-Ann noticed.

"Dude!" Lily-Ann cried. "That's a total Mongo!"

I hopped off and kicked the skateboard up into my hands. "What? You skate?"

She shook her head and looked down, smiling. Her blonde curls fell in front of her face. "No, but I know people who do, I guess."

"Oh, you do?" Jade asked.

Lily-Ann raised her hands. "Guilty as charged," she said lightly.

"You seem to have a lot going on that people don't know about," Jade said.

"I . . . um . . ." Lily-Ann shot Megan a pleading look. "I don't know what to say?"

Megan retreated into the Megan Clamshell.

I was at a loss for words, too. I stared at Jade for the umpteenth time.

"Better to keep your mouth shut and let people think you're an idiot, than open it and remove all doubt," Megan stated.

Lily-Ann started cracking up. "It's a Mark Twain quote!" she exclaimed.

Megan grabbed Lily-Ann's arm and hustled her toward the end of the boardwalk. "I have to show Lily-Ann downtown," she muttered in a distinctly un-Megan-like voice. "She's going to love it. Calypso, Prada, Gucci . . ." They disappeared around the corner, onto Main Street.

Jade's face looked like an old beach towel.

"I can't take the Jupiter Bounce anymore," Jade said. "I think I need to stop working. Why work? Why not plot our escape from this heinous town? Everyone is being corrupted. Even Megan."

"Jade, come on. Lily-Ann isn't so bad."

"She isn't?"

I gulped. "Well, think of some of the other tourists Megan has had to work for. Maybe you *both* should switch jobs."

Jade glanced at her watch. "That would be great, except that I got fired from my first job, and nearly got Megan fired, too, by association. Speaking of which, I better get back to work. Sarah's gonna get pissed."

"Jade, you're lying."

"Why do you think I'm lying?"

"Because Sarah isn't even *there*." I nodded toward Amusement Alley. The gates were still padlocked. "You're a better liar than that."

"What, do you know everything about me?"

I shook my head nervously. "Not by a long shot."

She took a deep breath. "Thank you. So stop giving me advice. Or name one thing you don't know about me. And it has to be big. Bigger than that I don't trust Lily-Ann Roth."

I wracked my crowded head. It was sort of like looking for a lost friend in a mosh pit; it was mostly shoving away. Not to make excuses, but it is a weird thing being asked what you *don't* know. All I could think of was what I *did* know: that she and Turquoise had different mothers whom neither of them had ever met (tourists, no doubt, who hooked up with Mr. Cohen during yoga instruction, isn't that "tantra"?); that her father was an unabashed hippie and was always struggling to make ends meet; that she had a crazy grandmother . . . and then, of course, the normal stuff; that she'd always stuck up for Megan; that she was stubborn to a fault; that she'd never say anything bad about anyone she loved, except Turquoise –

Suddenly, it hit me.

"Why did your father name you guys after gemstones, anyway?"

She giggled. "Are you serious?"

"Yes! And don't tell me 'because he's a freak.'"

"I never told you? *He* never told you? Well . . . it's not because he's a freak, even though he is. It's because of our eyes. He named us after the color of our eyes."

I didn't quite believe her, so I took the opportunity to jam her skateboard back into my backpack. "But you both have brown eyes."

"Yeah, but when Turkey was born, she had these really beautiful blue eyes."

"Wow. I can't believe you said 'beautiful' and 'Turkey' in the same sentence," I marveled, with just a hint of sarcasm.

Jade gave me a blank stare. "You've been to our house at Thanksgiving."

I laughed. "That's the Jade I know. So what about you? Why Jade?"

"I had green eyes. Come on, Miles. I've shown you my baby pictures. I actually showed them to you *at* Thanksgiving. Last year, remember? I had these bright green eyes when I was an infant."

"So what happened? Why do you both have brown eyes now?"

She sighed and touched my arm without looking at me. "We changed, Miles. It happens." Then she turned and walked back toward Amusement Alley.

Jade

I arrived home at around six P.M. — starving and disheveled after an insane day full of screaming toddlers — only to find Megan and Turquoise sitting at our kitchen table, poring over some article on Turquoise's laptop. *Megan has been replaced by an alien,* I thought, *roaming around town with Lily-Ann Roth and now looking up God-knows-what with Turquoise.*

Turquoise had also undergone some sort of radical transformation this year. I really hadn't noticed it until that moment. I *couldn't* have noticed. We were proverbial ships passing in the night, which was fine. But her perky little prepster outfits were gone. The crisp pants, the spotless white tops — the whole professional look . . . she'd traded them in for something . . . boho? She wore a long skirt, sandals, and some sort of psychedelic concert T-shirt (Aquarium Rescue Unit?) which screamed, in a word, Dad. She'd also lost weight and gotten color. How, I don't know. She looked frighteningly like me.

I closed the door behind me. I closed it pretty hard.

Turquoise and Megan turned at the same time.

"Hey, Jade," they announced in unison.

Then they turned back to the computer screen, deep in concentration.

"Hey, guys," I said with equal nonchalance. "So, I meant to tell you. I've decided to get that sex-change operation.

Also, there was a thermonuclear explosion on the beach. Anybody up for some din-din? Lobster rolls?"

Turquoise peered at me over her shoulder. "What did you just say?"

"Nothing."

"Don't joke about the beach," Turquoise said with a sigh. "This thing is real."

"What thing? Aside from everyone's insanity?"

"Insanity?" she repeated.

Now it was my turn to sigh. I flopped down in the chair beside them, too exhausted to go on. "Please explain to your dumb sister what you're talking about."

"Arnold Roth is planning to make some sort of announcement about the boardwalk. He's going to do it at Clam-Fest. He and his pretty little daughter really do want to tear it down."

Megan shook her head and folded her arms across her chest. "Lily-Ann has nothing to do with it. But you know why I'm really mad?" she grumbled, nodding at the computer. "That he's using Lily-Ann. And that he's using Clam-Fest as the platform. Like he's a . . . he's a . . ."

"Like he's a local," Turquoise concluded.

"Exactly," Megan said.

"So, what's the difference between him and you, Turkey?" I asked.

She spun around and smirked. "Excuse me, Jade?"

"You're not a local, either," I said. I stood and lumbered

over to the refrigerator, scouring for leftovers. Classic. There was nothing but salad (hers) and pizza (mine) — and the salad was getting that scary grayish color it does when it's been sitting on a shelf for over a week. "This is only the second time you've been back in two years. Even tourists come back more often than you do. Like Sean Edwards. He visited at Christmas."

"Did you see Sean today?" Megan asked. Her voice had an edge.

I closed the fridge door. My appetite suddenly vanished. "Um . . . no. Why? Is he back in town?"

"Yes, he's back in town," Megan said. "And he looks fantastic. He's changed."

I raised my hands, trying to make a joke. "Okay . . . I . . . I didn't know," I stammered. "I'm just —"

"Trying to make us feel stupid for caring about something," Megan cut in. "Because Jade Cohen doesn't care about anything, least of all this dump of a town. Right? You said it yourself a million times. All you want to do is leave here."

My eyes widened. For one of the first times ever, I was at a loss for words. "Meg, why are you mad at me?" I finally managed.

"I'm mad because you don't care. We happened to grow up in a town where if you're a local, you're an outsider. Well now *we* outsiders are fighting against the insiders, who aren't the locals. So are you in or are you out? Sounds to me like you're out. You always have been."

My lips quivered. "Meg . . . this can't be about the board-walk. And if outsiders are fake insiders, why is Lily-Ann your new best friend?"

She didn't answer.

"Hey, you guys," Turquoise murmured. "Let's all just calm down. Things might not be as dire as they seem. Maybe this Roth guy wants to tear down the boardwalk so he can build his daughter an even *better* boardwalk. Huh? Huh?"

I laughed. Another first: laughing at one of my sister's jokes. It was a day of firsts all around, but most of them pretty crappy. I stepped toward Megan.

She whirled and stormed out of the kitchen. "Bye, you guys. Turquoise, I'll talk to you later."

The front door slammed behind her.

I stared at Turquoise. "Why is Meg so pissed at me?" I asked. My heart thumped. "Did she tell you something? Do you know something?"

Does she know something?

"Something about what?"

Something about what happened between Miles and me, I wanted to say, but I shrugged instead.

She turned back to the computer. "All I know is that she thinks her best friend should care more about this town."

I frowned. Neither of us said anything for a while.

"Why don't you read these controversial articles at our local library?" I finally asked in the silence. "I understand it's very quiet. Fewer arguments. Plus, online porn."

"How about this?" Turquoise said, keeping her back to

me. "I promise to read at the library if you promise to take the garbage out for once in your life. It's starting to stink."

"Whatever you say, Turkey."

"Don't call me that."

"Whatever you say, Turkey," I repeated.

"Jade!" she yelled, still furiously pretending to read whatever was on-screen. I glimpsed the faint beginnings of a smile on her lips.

"Don't call me Jade," I said. "Call me . . . hmm. How about Dwarfish Emo Chick?"

She turned to me, but I dashed out of the kitchen before she could respond.

I kept running. I ran out the back door and collapsed into the sand with the sunset behind me. And once I caught my breath, I found myself missing Dad for the first time since he'd left. (Yet *another* first. Ugh.) I cried a little, too. Megan must have found out what happened. Miles must have told her. Like Dad, he *too* was honest to a fault. It was a mistake. I should have told her a long time ago.

Luckily nobody saw me crying, other than some random gray-haired tourist woman, strolling barefoot on the beach with her sandals in one hand. I watched the seagulls circle overhead. They reminded me of an illustrated children's story Dad used to read me a long time ago, about a bunch of birds in New York City . . . and how one got lost. I think they were ducks. Or turkeys. Some kind of bird.

I felt a lot like that right now.

Megan

I suppose I should explain my little freak-out.

I didn't even realize what caused it until Turquoise called me late that night (11:45; I was in bed watching *The Colbert Report*). Apparently, right after I'd stomped out, Turquoise had spotted Jade out the kitchen window, crying on the beach. Turquoise didn't want to interfere.

Instead, about an hour later, once the sun had set, Jade returned and took a shower. They ordered in more pizza and salad and fought over what music to listen to while they ate. (Jade argued for the Beatles — a pretty random call; she seemed much more into Daft Punk these days — and Turquoise argued for Phish.)

Then Jade fell asleep on the couch.

"I think she's jealous of this Lily-Ann girl," Turquoise whispered cautiously over the phone. "You know, since you've made friends with her. But, ah . . . and I don't mean to pry, but is everything okay between you guys? Did Jade do something?"

I shook my head, my throat tightening.

"Megan?"

"No, it's — I don't know," I croaked. "I'm just worried about the boardwalk thing. I guess I'm just mad that Jade isn't."

Turquoise kept quiet.

I was lying, though. I knew it. It made me feel sick. I began to sweat; my stomach turned — because of the secret I'd kept from myself: *I'm jealous of Jade's relationship with Miles.* The whole stupid show with Lily-Ann on the boardwalk this morning . . . that was just my attempt to try to act as comfortable with someone as Jade was with Miles. Which also fed the problem. Jade was equally as comfortable with *both* Miles and me. Why wasn't I as comfortable with Miles? Oh, right. Because I was in love with him, and Jade wasn't. It made perfect sense and it made no sense at all.

"That's really why you're mad?" Turquoise said. It didn't sound so much like a question, though. It sounded more like she was calling me on my BS.

"I'll take the fifth, Counselor," I muttered.

"Megan, I'm worried about the boardwalk thing, too," Turquoise said in a sympathetic tone. "But I'm more worried about Jade. She just seems . . . more lost than she's been in a while. And I also realize that she has a point: It's not fair of me to talk about her or criticize her, because I haven't been home in a while. I *am* like a tourist."

"No, you're not," I answered automatically.

She snickered.

"What?"

"Megan, when was the last time I called you? I'm really not a local. But you and Jade are. You're the best friend my sister could possibly have. And you never have a bad word to say about anyone. Not even losers like Sean Edwards. So what's going on?"

There was a nutty irony. Because for a second, I felt closer to Jade than I'd felt all summer long. Turquoise *was* nosy, and pushy, and self-righteous. I could just picture Jade making a crack about how Turquoise always used reverse psychology to make somebody feel stupid. (*"Classic wannabe lawyer move,"* she'd say.)

"Nothing is going on," I muttered. "I just had a lousy day."

"That's what Jade said."

"Ha, ha." I yawned. "Listen, Turquoise, I don't want to —"

"So are you guys serious about this pact party thing?" Turquoise asked, lowering her voice.

I sat up straight in bed, suddenly very wide-awake. I grabbed the remote and turned the TV off. "You know about the pact party?" I hissed.

"I'm not deaf, Megan," she said, and I knew she was smiling. "I hear things, even when I'm studying for the bar exam. The walls are pretty thin in this bungalow."

"Well . . ."

"If Jade is depressed about something, maybe this pact party could be just what the doctor ordered. We invite a bunch of tourists, and the usual crew from town — Brian Ashe and whoever else — and you and Miles and Jade will hang back, watching everybody try not to hook up, and you'll have a ball. And hopefully Jade will snap out of her funk. I can play the shrewish older sister."

I laughed out loud.

"What?" she said.

"Nothing. I um . . . that's just . . . nice. What I'd pay for Jade to be in on this conversation. I wish we were being wiretapped."

"She'd never believe it," Turquoise stated. "And don't joke about wiretapping."

"Hey, you're the lawyer. You know more about this stuff than I do."

"So do we have a deal? Pact party this weekend?"

I nodded. "We do indeed have a deal. Let's say Saturday —"

"MEGAN!" Mom yelled from her bedroom. "GET OFF THE PHONE AND GO TO BED! YOU HAVE TO CLEAN THE ROTHS' HOUSE TOMORROW!"

Party time indeed.

Part Three
The Pact Party

Jade

Megan and Lily-Ann were the first to arrive for the pact party, and they arrived together — which didn't exactly fill me with glee. To Megan's credit, however, she'd not only called me four times since our fight (if that's even what it was), but had also e-mailed, texted, and stuffed a handwritten note into our mail slot.

Hey, Jade, I am so sorry about the way I acted the other day. I guess I'm just stressed about the boardwalk situation, and about college applications, and about the summer . . . and blah, blah, blah. Anyway, very psyched for the big party! So is Turquoise! xoxoxo Your true BFF, Megan. P.S. You can't ever possibly get rid of me, even if you tried.

I was happy about that, I admit. Even though I got the feeling she was holding something back. Namely, that she knew about Miles and me.

What I still wasn't happy about was that Megan had clearly engaged in secret phone conversations with my sister, and that Turquoise had taken her sisterly new hippie vibe beyond the style phase and into the realm of reality. Where was the ice-cold condescension? Where were the complaints about my crappy attitude, appearance, and diet? Not that I missed that stuff . . . or did I?

But what bothered me the most was that Megan and *Lily-Ann* still seemed to be peas in a pod.

Exhibit A: In addition to showing up together, they also showed up with perfect makeup, hair parted in the middle, wearing black spaghetti-strap tops and short white skirts, and both carrying large ceramic bowls covered in Saran Wrap. With Megan's dark hair and Lily-Ann's flaxen waves, they looked like a photo and its negative.

"Hey, Jade!" Lily-Ann exclaimed.

"Hi." I peered at their bowls. Both were filled with some sort of red punch.

Megan gave me a kiss on the cheek. She smelled like expensive perfume.

"You look really cute," Lily-Ann remarked. "I love that dress."

I glanced down at myself. I hadn't even remembered what I'd thrown on — only that it was an easy something-or-other to go over my bathing suit, something I could whip off in case people wanted to splash around in the ocean later. I was hoping they would. Better to keep the riffraff outside than allow them to roam our house freely . . . and now that I looked at it, it wasn't cute at all. It was a horrible blue sundress with beads on the skirt that Dad had bought me for my fifteenth birthday.

"Thanks," I mumbled.

"Here, let me take that," Turquoise said, breezing past me and grabbing the bowl from Lily-Ann's arms. "Nice to meet you. I'm Jade's sister, Turquoise. Welcome to the Cohen household. I'd welcome you, too, Megan, but what's the point?"

"Um . . . that punch isn't spiked with anything, is it?" I asked as they stepped into the kitchen.

"Ha, ha, ha," Turquoise snorted. "Lily-Ann made it. Why don't you help out and be a host, and then you can taste for yourself."

At the very least, Turkey sounded like herself again. "How do you know Lily-Ann made the punch?" I asked.

"Megan told me," Turquoise said absently, grabbing a soup ladle from the drawer.

"Oh," I said.

Megan and Lily-Ann exchanged a quick glance, the sort of glance Miles and I would exchange whenever the conversation veered dangerously close to our secret.

Turquoise joined the glancing, too. Yes, the pact party was off to a great start.

"Megan called to ask what she should bring, and Lily-Ann offered to make some punch," Turkey explained. "Now will you stop standing around like a basket case and help out a little? Turning our humble little home into the Jade Cohen party house was *your* idea, if I'm not mistaken."

Touché. Turkey was definitely back. And I was strangely glad. I opened the pantry and scooped out some long rolls of plastic cups. Turkey stirred Megan's bowl of punch. "So what's in there, anyway?" I asked.

"Vitamin water and vodka," Lily-Ann responded. "Power C."

"Vodka?" I asked, staring at Turkey.

Lily-Ann nodded. "Just a splash. My dad gets vodka sent specially from Iceland or something. I figured, what the hell? He didn't seem to mind. It isn't all that much. Less than a quarter bottle for each bowl."

"Great!" I beamed as broadly as I could. "Turkey? Are you okay with all of this? Serving booze to a bunch of kids?"

"I'm not a kid," she said casually. She kept stirring. "And since when did *you* become a lawyer? It's not like I'll get disbarred. I haven't even taken the exam." She raised her eyes and grinned.

Megan and Lily-Ann giggled.

"Oh," I said. "Well, this is nice. It'll mark the very first time I've gotten drunk in my life. I'm glad I can share it with my darling sister, my best friend . . . and a perfect stranger. Dad would be so proud! Should we call him and let him know?"

Lily-Ann shook her head. "You won't get drunk," she said firmly. "I promise. There's barely anything in there."

I rolled my eyes. "I feel so much better. You're right. I think I'll have a cup."

"Anyway, I'm not a perfect stranger. I'm your best friend's *employer.*"

I gazed down at the bowls. Megan had grabbed a wooden spoon out of the cupboard and had begun to stir her own drink. I wondered if Miles would indulge. Why not? He'd already indulged in sharing our secret. At least, I was pretty sure he had.

But no, this was the pact party. The whole point was abstinence. Right?

I tore open a cylinder of plastic cups, snatched one out, and scooped up some punch — drenching my hand in the process. I leaned back and chugged as rapidly as possible. It tasted acrid, sweet, and poisonous.

So much for abstinence.

Miles

I knew this was party was a lousy idea. I knew it as soon as I turned the corner onto Ocean Street. Brian Ashe, Sean Edwards, and I all happened to arrive at the same time: Sean, by BMW; Brian, by dirt bike; me, by skateboard.

Plus, there was the weather. A storm was coming. It felt like the night of August 11 last year. On humid overcast evenings, the Cohens' remote beachside block tends to smell more of dead crabs than sand . . . and the cozy bungalows tend to look a little more gray and depressed than usual . . . *Bad karma*, as Jade's dad might say.

"Dude!" Brian shouted. He was rapping on the front door. "Caught you skateboarding on the boardwalk the other day! Bold move with your gimp leg!"

"Thanks, Brian!" I shouted back.

"So, is your leg, like, permanently damaged?"

"Hey," Sean chimed in before I could respond.

"Hey, Sean," I said. *Funny*, I thought. For once, I liked the guy. Maybe it was because he'd finally decided to dress like a normal human being (disregarding the seashell necklace) — whereas Brian had donned a suit jacket, jeans, and wifebeater T-shirt combo. It was old-school *Miami Vice*, gone completely wrong.

"Why *are* you dressed like that?" I decided to ask Brian. I couldn't really help it.

He clapped me on the back and turned the knob. "Door's open!" He kicked it ajar with his foot and strolled — or, I guess pimp-rolled — inside. "I heard that this was a no-hooking-up party, Bro. You and your weird chick friends came up with the idea. Another bold move! Just trying to look as nasty as possible."

I turned to Sean.

"Me, too?" he said, sounding bewildered. "Megan invited me. You know, because we both work at the Roth place —"

"Hey, guys!"

Jade lurched into view, clutching the door frame, dressed in a bikini.

I blinked at her. She never wore bikinis; she was strictly one-piece. She laughed loudly. Her teeth were pink, as if she'd been drinking Kool-Aid. I forced myself not to look at her body. Her eyes were a little glassy.

Sean waved at her and quickly scurried in after Brian. "Thanks for the invite."

"Welcome to the punch party, Miles," Jade murmured.

"You mean *pact* party, right?" I leaned forward and sniffed. "Are you drunk or something? You smell weird. Where's Turquoise?"

Jade rolled her eyes and stumbled after Sean, her bare feet smacking on the front hall tile floor. "Always the charmer, Miles. Turkey's even drunker than I am." Her voice was lost in the din of laughter and some monotonous hip-hop drumbeat.

I glanced back at my skateboard. It sat on the little patch

of dried grass next to the cobbled brick walkway. I could easily hop back on it and ride back home. I wondered what Megan would think when she found out I'd bailed on the pact party.

A hand clamped down on my shoulder.

I turned around, hoping to see Megan. It was Lily-Ann Roth.

"Hi," I said, feeling heat cross my cheeks. *Damn.*

"Hi back." She waved a cup in my face, her blue eyes boring into my own. "Come on in, Miles Gordon. It's your pact party. You can cry if you want to."

I bit the inside of my cheek.

Keeping myself from staring at Jade's body was one thing; keeping myself from staring at Lily-Ann's wasn't possible. The hair, the manicured toenails, the miniskirt, the black bikini top, the stomach, the belly button ring . . . She was the classic perfect tourist. And I was so, so attracted to her.

"What do you mean, I can cry if I want to?" I heard myself ask.

Lily-Ann sneered. "You've never heard that song?"

Get on the skateboard now.

"Um, no. I haven't."

"Oh, well, Turquoise put it on," Lily-Ann muttered. "I think she's a little tipsy." She waved her cup back toward the music, spilling a little as she did so. It landed on the floor with a bright red splat.

I peered inside. "Um . . . why aren't any of the girls here wearing shirts?"

"Ha!" Lily-Ann hiccuped. "Jade said that everybody who was wearing a bathing suit under their shirts had to take off their shirts. She wants us all to dive into the ocean later. And that was pretty much . . . everybody." Lily-Ann leaned closer. I could smell her shampoo on her blonde curls. It smelled a lot better than what was in her cup. "I think Jade might be a little tipsy, too," she whispered.

I drew back. "What about you? Not that you're slurring your words or anything, but you strike me as less than sober right now." I jerked a finger straight up at the sky. "And even though it's cloudy, the sun still hasn't gone down. Isn't it a little early to be hitting the sauce?"

"No it isn't, *D-A-A-A-D*," Jade retorted, cocking her eyebrow at me. "Why don't you relax and have a cocktail? Seashell Point is a 'resort town,' isn't it? That's what my dad says, anyway. And he should know. My mom thinks he's Satan."

Mom and Dad issues, all in one, I thought. *Just like me.*

At least, Megan and Jade only had one of each. But Lily-Ann and I . . . we had both. My mom occasionally thought my dad was Satan, too — especially when he suggested that I take truck-driving lessons "because it's an important skill to have." I imagine it would be, if one wanted to drive a truck for a living. He said this to me when I was still in the ICU. Translation: *Son, you're clearly a moron, so why don't you set your sights a little lower?* Thank God, Mom told him to shut up.

"Well, everybody's parents are Satan every now and then," I said — only because I was a little self-conscious about the long stretch of quiet between us.

Lily-Ann laughed. "Everyone's kid can be Satan, too. Like me."

"What is that supposed to mean?"

"It means: Why don't you come in and have a drink? It's not like we're gonna hook up. It's the pact party, remember?" She turned and beckoned me toward the kitchen, through a dancing mob of tourists.

Once again, I tried not to look at her body.

Megan

I really did want to stay away from the punch. The only problem was that once Jade started . . . I don't know. It seemed to me that whenever somebody wanted to communicate with someone in an altered state (as Lily-Ann might say) and God knew, I'd been having trouble communicating with Jade lately — the person would have to assume an altered state, too. So I drank the punch. I drank it because I wanted to talk to Jade. Really *talk* to her. She still hadn't quite accepted my apology. I couldn't blame her.

At first, the punch tasted gross, like drinking cough medicine. Lily-Ann justified the health hazard by saying, "Everyone has their vices. I mean, just ask Miles. My dad goes to his clam shack literally every afternoon. Do you know how bad those fried clams are for you?"

Halfway through the second cup, I began to feel pretty good. I found myself smiling at all the tourist girls, jigging around the Cohens' tiny bungalow and the patio deck in their bikini tops. I found myself staring at Sean Edwards a few times, too. He was so much *cuter* now. Or was he? I mean, he'd let his chestnut-brown hair grow, and his necklace was dumb . . . but suddenly he was way more Seth Cohen than preteen boy-toy. And so far, things had been fine at the Roths' house while I was cleaning. He was totally diligent about the gardening job. He stuck to the greenhouse. At first, I thought it was because he was being rude and trying to avoid me . . . but I wondered if he was just being cool about it all.

He caught me staring at him. I waved, blushing. He walked over.

"Everything all right?" he asked.

"Yeah, I just want to know why you never come in to say hi when we work."

"Because it's work," he said with a chuckle.

I peeked at his cup. The liquid in it was clear, not red.

"What's that?" I asked.

"Water."

"Really?"

"Yup." He glanced at some of the tourists, dancing around us — all with their hands in the air. "I thought about drinking some punch. But when I heard a couple of people say 'Dude, this house is so ghetto!' I decided not to."

I gazed into his twinkling blue eyes. "When did you become so nice?"

"I don't know," he said in a dry voice. "Maybe after I decided that it wasn't cool to be some tourist jerk who hits on local chicks. Hey, Megan, are you sure you're okay?" He reached for my cup. "How about you have some water instead?"

I yanked the cup away from his hands. "No way, José."

"José?" He laughed again. His long hair flopped in his eyes, the way Miles's used to, before the accident. "Man. Jade's dad goes away for the summer and suddenly everyone goes completely —" He stopped in mid-sentence, staring over my shoulder.

"Completely?" I prodded.

"Nuts!" Jade shrieked behind me, poking me in the back.

I nearly dropped my drink. "Don't do that! You scared me."

"Sorry."

She smiled at Sean. She'd lost her sundress. I'd never seen her so scantily clad in my life. Where did she get that bikini? But best not to ask. She looked hot, though . . . no doubt: small, tan, curvy, and perfect. Her hair was a little frizzy, but other than that — I noticed that Sean noticed, too. Of course, he did; he was a guy. I was almost mad. Jade was always ragging on me because she claimed I wasn't as hot as *I* realized? I thought about dishing some of her own dirt back at her — but then I had a better idea.

"Hey, what's the theme of this party again, Jade?" I asked.

"Abstinence," she said.

I giggled and punched her arm. She giggled and punched back. To this day, I still won't admit I was drunk. I couldn't have been drunk. I was just mildly loopy.

"We were in a fight, but we made out," Jade announced to Sean, as if this would somehow explain our psychotic behavior.

Sean tilted his head away from us. His eyes narrowed. "What did you just — ?"

"I mean we made *up*," Jade groaned.

"Well, then why don't you break the rules?" I asked. "Parties are made for breaking things, right? You did invite — yikes — *tourists*."

"Like me, right?" Sean frowned between the two of us.

Jade and I both laughed again.

"Right on," Jade said. "And speaking of which, why did you get a job working in the Roths' greenhouse? What tourist *works* over the summer?"

He shook his head. "I wanted to . . . I don't know. Do something for once. Be productive. Avoid my parents and their dumb parties." He drained his cup, and then turned toward the door. "Thanks, Jade —"

"No, wait!" Jade held up her hands. "Sean, I'm sorry. Please stay. I really want to know why you got a job working in that greenhouse. I didn't even know you were into gardening."

He tossed the empty cup into the Cohens' umbrella stand.

(To his credit, it was empty, so the stand looked like a garbage can. To Jade's credit, she didn't mention it. Or maybe she didn't even see. Her eyes were glued to his, and besides, everyone had grabbed all the umbrellas, because it was starting to drizzle.)

"I am," he said. "I've really gotten into plants recently. Well, just generally . . . I've gotten into conservation and environmentalism."

"You have?" Jade murmured. "How come you never talk about it?"

"When do you and I talk, Jade?" he asked, grinning the way she would grin.

"Good point," she said. "Meg, what was that movie you tried to make me watch after all the sheep escaped from Pete's Petting Zoo? You know, the one where Brad Pitt looked crazy and ugly? *That* was about animals, too . . . wasn't it? It was called *Twelve Something. Twelve Uglies.*"

Sean started to laugh.

"What?" Jade asked.

"The Roths just got that movie on Netflix," he murmured. "*Twelve Monkeys.*"

"You guys should go watch it right now," I said, without thinking. "The Roths are out to dinner with my mom. The wide-screen LCD would be all yours."

My heart blossomed. *Then I can have Miles to myself. Maybe.*

Jade and Sean looked at each other. Then they smiled at the floor flirtatiously, as if they should be smiling at each other. I was the happiest I'd been all night.

"Well I kind of wanted to split anyway," Sean said under his breath.

"Me, too!" Jade giggled, ran to the front hall closet, grabbed an old yellow raincoat, and slipped it over her bikini. "I mean, it's raining, which is always bad for a party."

Amen, Jade Cohen, I thought — chuckling to myself as the door swung shut behind them. *Amen, indeed . . . because Sean is a very, very good kisser. Also, conveniently, Miles is still here. And now maybe I can finally figure out why you have both been acting so strangely.*

Miles

"So, Miles, what really happened last summer?" Lily-Ann whispered. She'd taken my hand and had begun stroking my fingers with her thumb, very lightly, in an undeniably sexy way. "You were in some surfing accident?"

I couldn't focus. "Yeah. It was ... I ... it was in the newspaper."

I searched the kitchen for Megan, who'd been busy chatting up Sean Edwards in a kind of a sexy way, as well. I couldn't see her anywhere. Jade was gone, too. Turquoise, on the other hand, in the spirit of her younger sister, had shed most of her clothing except for her bathing suit. She was waving a cup of punch, twirling around among a bunch of blonde tourists who bore an uncanny resemblance to Lily-Ann, only with straighter hair. I recognized a few of them from the boardwalk. But I also felt like I didn't. They could have been cloned from the same gene pool. Maybe they had been. The tourists seemed to look more and more alike every year ... it sounds awful, but at that moment, I *was* burning to get out of Seashell Point.

"I can't believe he does that," Lily-Ann said, squeezing my hand. "It is totally, totally inappropriate."

"You can't believe who does what?"

"That my dad swings by Sonny's every afternoon to buy

clams, even though he's gonna tear down the boardwalk. Guilt. He's great at guilt."

We'd been talking about that?

"Maybe he just likes the clams," I murmured.

"Whatever. Totally inappropriate," she repeated.

I grinned. "Inappropriate? That sounds like a word *my* dad would use."

She laughed and set her cup down on the counter, then took my other hand. "You're a total cutie-pie; you know that, right?"

"I'm a . . . what?"

"A cutie-pie. Why don't you have a girlfriend?"

A girlfriend?

Okay. As a guy? When a hot, smart, glamorous girl uses the words *cutie-pie* and *girlfriend* with you — in the interrogative — something happens. Your brain shuts down. I could think of a dozen different reasons why I didn't have a girlfriend, mostly revolving around a complete lack of self-confidence after my accident/recovery/stupidity . . . but I decided to keep quiet instead.

"Why don't we go outside?" Lily-Ann whispered. "I like swimming in the rain."

"Mm-hmm," I answered, my heart starting to pound.

All of a sudden, the music died.

A collective *"aww"* followed.

Turquoise barreled into the kitchen, an off-kilter grin on her lips. "Okay, people!" she shouted. "The pact party is officially over!"

"Why?" Lily-Ann asked, still clinging to both my hands. "Because it's raining?"

"No, because I just caught Brian Ashe making out with Cindy . . . Cindy . . ." She tapped her lip and chuckled. "I don't know. Cindy Tourist. The one from London? The point is: They were making out in my bed. So the party can go on, but the pact part is over. And the much more important part: STAY OUT OF MY FREAKING BEDROOM, UNLESS YOU WISH LIFETIMES OF FUTURE LITIGATION! I'M IN LAW SCHOOL, PEOPLE! I MEAN IT —"

The music blared back on at twice the volume. It drowned out Turquoise's voice.

Everybody cheered.

Lily-Ann laughed. I had to laugh, too. She squeezed me against her, and I closed my eyes. My hands lingered on the small of her back. Her lips gently brushed my neck.

"Lily-Ann," I started. "I . . ."

"What?" she breathed.

"I don't think . . . I don't think . . ." I wanted to add: *That this is a good idea. I think I want to find Megan.* I thought it, but I didn't say it. I did want Lily-Ann after all. And the pact was over.

"I'm glad," she murmured. She pulled me in closer, reaching her fingers under the back of my T-shirt. She kissed my neck again. Her curls tickled my shoulder. "I don't think, either."

I swallowed, remembering what Jade had said, even as I

began to kiss Lily-Ann's neck. *"The last thing I want do this summer is think. No thinking at all."*

We stumbled outside together, heading for the pool. The rain was coming down in thick, cold drops. No one else was in the pool; a few kids were huddled under the awning, sipping punch and sharing cigarettes. I felt strange, surreal, myself, but not myself. Maybe this was the new Miles, the postaccident Miles. Sure, I'd kissed tourist girls in the past, but I'd always joked about it with Megan and Jade later. Now, this felt different.

The rain was freezing on my chest as I took off my T-shirt. Lily-Ann shed her miniskirt, revealing the teeny black bottom of her bikini. *Good Lord.*

At the same time, we dove into the pool. I submerged and, for a split second, felt that small squeeze of fear, the fear of drowning that I'd never, ever had before the accident. Jade, Megan, and I were like little fish growing up, dipping and bobbing through the waves without a hint of worry. Maybe growing up is about learning to get scared.

And then I surfaced and Lily-Ann kissed me. For real. She hung her wet arms around my neck and put her mouth on mine, and I felt up and down her curves and kissed her hungrily as the rain poured down on us. Everything was wet. There were no thoughts. I kissed Lily-Ann's throat, and she kissed my ear. I felt so good. And then, for no reason at all, I thought: *Megan.*

I have no idea why. I suppose I should have thought of

Jade, since she was the last girl I had kissed. But all I could think of was Megan, her dark eyes, and her silence, and the way she wanted to be mayor of Seashell Point.

And then, just like that, there she was, standing at the entrance to the pool, soaking and shivering in her little bikini. Staring at me and Lily-Ann. Instinctively, I pulled away from Lily-Ann and I heard her make a confused, annoyed sound. But I could only look at Megan.

She had on her face the same shocked expression that Jade had worn when she first saw my twisted, swollen leg. And just like Jade had done that time, Megan turned and bolted.

Jade

I swear I wasn't really all that drunk. I mean I don't even know what drunk *feels* like, because I've never been drunk before.

What I do know is this: About three minutes after we left, Sean Edwards remembered that he didn't have the keys to the Roths' house. Well, he had the keys to the *greenhouse*, but not the mansion. And if we were going to watch this movie, he needed said keys. What I also know: Sean Edwards wasn't nearly the loser tourist I'd thought he was. Maybe it was the rain or his scruffy new look (he sure wore the whole bohemian thing *way* better than Turquoise), but he'd actually managed to charm me. Environmentalism? Conservation? A year ago, I would have sworn on a stack of Bibles that the guy didn't even know how to *spell* those words.

"We've got to get the keys from Megan or Lily-Ann," he whispered.

"But how?" I asked.

"Well, I'm sure Megan will give them right up, because she was the one who said we should watch the movie in the first place on the Roths' fat TV screen."

He meant to say flat. We both cracked up.

I wrapped my arm around his waist as we tiptoed back to my house. The rain made his T-shirt cling to his chest; I could see his smooth chest and abs underneath. He definitely had something going on. He might not have been a gorgeous rock star, but . . .

"Jade, are you sure you're not drunk?" he asked out of the blue.

"Of course!" I cried. I led him around back, across the patchy lawn — where Miles's skateboard still lay, now soaked by the rain — to the screen door that opened onto the beach. We stumbled a bit in the sand. His fingers interlocked with mine, tightening my hand on his hip.

Where the *hell* was this going?

I stopped short when we reached the screen door. Somebody had knocked it off track; it hung sideways like a picture that had fallen out of its frame. Not only that, somebody had blown out the bug-repelling candles in big scented buckets I'd strategically placed by the door (okay, maybe the rain had extinguished them, but still, I wanted to blame the tourist kids), so now there were flies buzzing into the house.

Dad would just love this.

The music thumped from inside. I heard shrieking and laughter and I didn't recognize a single voice.

Sean let my hand go. "Wow," he said. "I hope your place doesn't get too trashed tonight. It was really cool of you to throw this party."

"It's Turkey's party now." I crept under the hanging door — and instantly spotted Megan's white skirt in the mudroom, tossed haphazardly onto our old worn couch. There were a lot of skirts down here. Everyone must have been out by the pool. Or upstairs.

I glanced toward the ocean and caught a glimpse of my reflection in the sliding glass door. (At least *that* wasn't broken.) It served as an unpleasant reminder that I was wearing a yellow overcoat and a bikini, one I'd swiped from Turquoise no less. My hair was plastered to my head from the rain. *Good Lord.* I looked like a serial killer. The only things missing were the night-vision goggles and cattle prod.

"Jade?" Sean whispered from outside. "Everything all right in there?"

"Yeah, yeah . . . let me just find . . ." I scurried over to Megan's skirt and fished through the pocket for the keys. A big chain rattled. I scooped them up and dangled them in front of my face, chuckling — then ran back outside.

Sean was staring at something down the beach.

He pointed a finger through the rain. It was Megan. She was running toward her house, away from the boardwalk and the mansions. Or, at least, I assumed she was running toward her house. Beyond our little community of bungalows on the outskirts of Seashell Point, there isn't much left, other than a dilapidated, out-of-service lighthouse, where people like Brian Ashe sniff glue or drink beer. I glanced at the keys again.

"Why is she leaving without her skirt and her top?" I asked. "She's shivering. Look at her. She's hugging herself. She looks freezing." All I wanted to do was chase after her.

Sean shook his head. "Maybe she wanted to change into something dry?"

Two other shadowy figures appeared in her wake. They'd emerged from the back door on the other side, where the pool was. And they weren't too hard to recognize. Nope. Even if there was a raging hurricane instead of a rainy, humid Seashell Point night, I could have recognized them: Lily-Ann and Miles. They were holding hands. They watched Megan as she disappeared into the rain . . . and then they turned to each other.

I held my breath.

They were *still* holding hands. Miles looked about a foot taller than she did —

Their lips met.

I kicked at the wet sand.

"What are you thinking?" Sean finally asked.

"Let's go watch that movie," I said.

Megan was right. Sean Edwards was a very good kisser. Not that he needed much encouragement to get the ball rolling.

We arrived at the beach entrance of the Roths' house (several sliding glass doors, as opposed to one with a broken screen), and both whispered to each other, "*Shhhhh*," fingers held to our mouths, staring at each other and laughing.

"You promise me you're not drunk?" Sean demanded for the thousandth time. "Because I know that I've had this reputation of being this slimy tourist —"

To shut him up, I gave him a quick peck on the lips. He pecked back and lingered for a while. I fumbled for the keys.

Even in the darkness, it wasn't hard to see that this place was a palace. It was a hell of a lot more luxurious than the Jupiter Bounce, and this mudroom was about twice as big as *ours*. Ironic: Dad and I called the room that led to the beach the mudroom because we always tracked wet sand in. It was where we kept our rattiest furniture, our oldest towels, and boxes of random unused crap, like Turquoise's high school valedictorian trophy. But either Megan was a better house-cleaner than I'd imagined, or the Roths were more anal, because a person could eat off this floor.

I glanced nervously at the antique furniture, a couch the size of my room, and lamps the size of trees. Instinctively, I ground my toes into the doormat.

Sean tiptoed over to a large cabinet, next to the flat-screen mounted on the wall.

"What are you doing?" I whispered.

"Fixing us a drink."

I giggled as he removed a large bottle of ginger ale and swished it in front of his face. "A-ha!" he exclaimed. "I knew it! Every tourist keeps a fully stocked liquor cabinet in the beach room. Just ask my parents. It even has caffeine — which is exactly what you need. You know, I think a lot of dumb things, and sometimes I'm right." He took his shirt off. He was nicely built, to say the least. "Sorry, it's just really wet, and I'm really cold from the rain."

I shook my head. "Don't apolo . . . apolo . . ."

He squinted at me. "Huh?"

"Put down the ginger ale, Sean." I ran forward and dove onto the couch. "Come here." I took off my raincoat and stretched across the pillows, grinning at him through the shadows. "I'm not thirsty."

"What about the movie?" he breathed in a husky voice.

"How about we entertain each other?"

He placed the bottle on the countertop and slunk over.

"Are you sure you're not — ?"

"Stop asking!"

I watched his chiseled, happy face get closer and closer, like a video close-up, until it filled my entire field of vision. I grabbed the back of his head and kissed him with all the pent-up desire that fueled my rock-star fantasies. Sean's kisses made me oddly trembly. And it didn't feel surreal, like when I'd kissed Miles last summer. It felt so right. Especially when he moved his hands along my collarbone, down to my belly button.

I couldn't wait to tell Megan —

The lights flew on.

I blinked. Sean scooted out of my arms. It was suddenly *very* bright.

"What the hell is going on down here?" a thunderous voice demanded.

Mr. Roth stood at the bottom of the stairwell at the far end of the room.

He was wearing that same ridiculous seersucker-and-blue-button-down combo he'd worn the first day we'd spotted him. I was tempted to giggle. Unfortunately, I was also tempted to pass out. He folded his arms across his chest, his jaw tightly set. "Sean, who is this girl, and why is she wearing a wet bikini on my couch? And why aren't you wearing a shirt? And why is the liquor cabinet open? And what the hell makes you think you can treat my home like your own private bordello? You're my *gardener*, for Christ's sake! What will your parents say when I tell them?"

Sean opened his mouth. Nothing came out.

"How did you get in here?" Mr. Roth barked.

"Megan gave me the keys," I answered on Sean's behalf. The words were slurred. It sounded more like: "*Megah-gave-uh-me-da-keys*," like a parody of an Italian accent. "I'm Jade, by the way. All this is my fault."

"I see," Mr. Roth snapped. "Interesting. Well, then, Megan Kim is fired."

"What?" I shouted, sitting up straight. If I'd been even the slightest bit tipsy, I definitely wasn't anymore. "She had nothing to do with this! She's always been the responsible one! I'm the one who got fired for this exact same thing two summers ago! I just told you —"

"Jade? It's Jade, correct?" Mr. Roth thrust his finger toward the sliding glass doors. "Young lady, I have no idea who you are or what you're doing in my home, but I'd like both you and Mr. Edwards to leave. Otherwise, I'm calling the police."

I snapped up my raincoat as Sean feverishly squirmed back into his damp T-shirt. But I couldn't help but think, *This isn't your home, jerk. It's a mansion you're renting in MY town — a town you want to rebuild in your own image.* For once, though, I decided to bite my tongue and keep these astute observations to myself. Sean and I blushed at each other. He looked away. I yanked open the door, sprinting back out onto the rain-drenched beach.

"One more thing," Mr. Roth called after us. "Mr. Edwards, just so we're clear? You're also fired. Stay away from my greenhouse."

And he slid the door shut.

Megan

Thank God, Mom wasn't home when I burst in, panting, dripping, nearly in tears, stinking of liquor — and, of course, wearing only my bathing suit. My head spun, but it wasn't the punch. (No, on second thought, it *was* the punch.) I shook my hair furiously, like a wet dog. Water splattered all over the front hall. I flicked on the lights and ran to the bathroom to grab a towel.

The bad part about being drunk? It feels good for maybe the first fifteen minutes . . . and then it just feels confusing and miserable and sickly.

Stupid move, I kept repeating to myself. *Stupid move to think I could actually trust and maybe even become friends with someone like Lily-Ann Roth.*

And it had nothing to do with the fact that Lily-Ann made out with Miles in front of me. It was like Turquoise said: The pact party was a disaster, a failure, a bomb. Anything could go at the Cohen sisters' party house, and it certainly had. No . . . what bothered me was that Lily-Ann swore to me that she hadn't put "much" vodka in the punch. At least, that's what I tried to convince myself was bothering me as I ran a towel through my hair and avoided looking at myself in the mirror.

As if I would even know how much was "much"? People wouldn't be stripping otherwise, would they? It was a typical manipulative, selfish, bubble-brained tourist move. Lily-Ann just hid her stupidity better than most. But, of course, she did. She'd made friends with her cleaning lady, because her cleaning lady happened to be best friends with the one boy-toy she *really* wanted, which wasn't her greenhouse gardener —

The phone rang.

"Great," I moaned.

I hurled the towel to the floor and stomped to my bedroom to pick it up. The caller ID read ROTH. At first I wasn't sure whether to laugh or scream.

"Lily-Ann, it's really not that big a deal," I groaned, skipping the hello and cutting right to the chase. I flopped back in bed. "I just I wasn't feeling well. The punch was stronger than you —"

"This isn't Lily-Ann."

I sat up. My eyes bulged. "Mr. Roth?" I whispered.

"Yes. I'm calling to tell you that you don't need to bother showing up to clean my house tomorrow, or any time after. You're fired. I'd also appreciate it if you stayed away from my daughter. Now will you please put your mother on?"

"I . . . I . . ." I stammered.

I wracked my brain for any plausible explanation as to why Mr. Roth would fire me. It didn't make any sense. He'd always laughed whenever he talked to me, telling me how thrilled he was that I'd befriended his daughter.

All I could think of was this one time when I'd accidentally thrown his silk bathrobe in the washing machine. It was hand-stitched, dry-clean only. But he'd even laughed about *that*, too. He'd said, "No worries; the shrinkage is in all the right places. I can wear it as a Hawaiian shirt now. *HAUGGH!*"

"Megan, your mother?" he snapped.

I shook my head. "She isn't here. I thought she was out to dinner with you. Look, this isn't about the Hawaiian bath-robe, is it? Because I'll totally buy you a new —"

"Megan, I'm home, which means I'm certain your mother is home, too."

Sure enough, as if he'd pulled some psychic trigger, I heard the front door open.

"Listen, Mr. Roth," I pleaded desperately. I jumped up and shut my bedroom door, cupping the phone around my hands and lowering my voice to a hiss. "I —"

"Megan," he interrupted. "I just spent a very unpleasant few minutes watching your drunken friends as they fondled each other on my couch. Apparently, all thanks to you and your handy set of my house keys, which I *en-trust-ed* to you." (He specially emphasized the "trust" part.) "NOW PUT YOUR MOTHER ON THE PHONE!"

I slammed the phone back down on the hook.

I couldn't help it.

I stared at the receiver.

What did I just do? Bad move. Jade was definitely right about one thing, this truly *was* the summer of no thinking.

"Megan, honey?" Mom called.

The phone began to ring again. I squeezed my eyes shut. But there was no point in postponing the inevitable. I steeled my nerves, forced my lids open, and snatched up the receiver. "Mr. Roth, I —"

"Meg, it's Jade."

I frowned. "Jade?"

"Is your caller ID screwed up?" She was sniffling. Her voice sounded scratchy.

"I . . . um, no. I didn't look. I guess I'm a little messed up tonight."

"Oh," she whispered.

Fear jabbed me. She was crying. "What's wrong?"

"I am so, so sorry. But I have something to tell you."

"You got me fired by making out with Sean Edwards in my boss's house, after raiding his liquor cabinet?" I said. I'd out-Jaded Jade herself.

Mom knocked on the door. "Megan?"

"Mom, just give me a second! I'm on the phone with Jade, okay?"

"Okay, but we need to talk," Mom answered. "I'll be in the kitchen."

Wonderful, I thought. *This is shaping up to be the greatest night of my life.*

Jade hadn't uttered so much as a peep. Now she was out-Megging me.

"Jade?" I said. "I don't have much time —"

"If it's the last thing I ever do on this planet, I am going to make it up to you," Jade sobbed. She drew in a deep shaky breath. "You can have every single cent I've ever made at the Jupiter Bounce. Not just this summer, either, but last summer and the year before that. Dad made me put it all in a savings account."

"Jade, I don't want your summer job money."

She sniffled again.

"Sorry, that came out wrong," I muttered.

"What *do* you want? Anything. Just tell me."

A vision of Miles drifted through my mind. A specific vision . . . the one I'd seen not too long ago: the way he'd swept Lily-Ann Roth into his arms and made out with her in the middle of the pool. In the rain.

But I didn't think Jade would ever be able to give me Miles. And for that reason, I sort of hated my best friend then.

Part Four
Clams

Miles

"Hello?" I said, gripping my cell phone. I stared at the glowing numbers on the clock next to my bed. It was nearly two in the morning. I was confused, guilt-ridden, and cotton-mouthed. (I guess that means hungover.) My leg hurt, too. It always hurt when it rained. Not to mention that the last thing I remembered clearly was kissing Lily-Ann good night . . . which now, for some reason, made me feel even *more* ill.

"He's doing it," Megan finally said. I could barely hear her.

"Who's doing what?" I asked. I remembered how stricken Megan had looked when she'd seen me kissing Lily-Ann. *Why* had she looked so upset? Because I'd broken the pact? Why did I *feel* so upset?

Unless —

"Mr. Roth is going to tear down the boardwalk, Miles."

"When did you find out?" I cleared my throat.

"Tonight. A few hours ago."

"He's going to tear down the boardwalk to build a dock?"

She let out a long sigh. "Yes, Miles. I can tell you a fourth time, if you'd like."

"But I just don't . . . I mean don't you understand what this means? If Arnold Roth tears down the boardwalk and builds a dock, jutting right out of Main Street, it'll completely ruin the surfing. It'll split the tide from where the waves break. Surfing will be over in this town, seriously. Seashell Point will be just some lame beach town. I mean, isn't that part of the draw for the tourists? The surfing? Your mom knows that. If that dock goes up, it'll be too dangerous, unless we want to pull what they did in *Dogtown and Z-boys*, surfing under the piers —"

"What do you care so much about surfing anymore, any-way?" Megan demanded.

Ouch. I scowled at the phone for a second.

Megan was acting totally un-Megan-like. It wasn't just the hour — the latest she'd ever called in the past was at midnight, tops, right after *The Colbert Report*. But the surfing jab was plain cruel. It was even too cruel for Jade, who pushed the cruelty envelope much harder than Megan ever had.

"What's that supposed to mean?" I asked, after I'd collected myself.

"You seem fine with skateboarding," she said. "So did the kids in that documentary. A documentary you wouldn't have seen if it weren't for me, by the way."

I scratched my wet, sandy scalp, desperately trying to get a grip on the conversation. "I never said I wouldn't . . . Megan, why are you pissed at me right now?" *Other than the fact that I broke the pact right in front of you.*

"I'm not pissed at *you*. I'm pissed at the stupid Roth family."

"Okay, okay." I lowered my voice, just in case my parents woke up.

"I mean, come on, Miles. My mom comes home, marches into the kitchen, and tells me that there's this crazy plan to tear down the boardwalk and build a dock that leads to a big 'floating casino.'" She let out a bitter little laugh. "The best part? They're gonna make the announcement at Clam-Fest. You should hear the name of the ship, too. It's perfect."

I held my breath. She kept quiet.

"Megan?"

"*The Royal We*," she said.

I started cracking up. I couldn't help it. "Are you serious?"

"That's why we're on the phone at two A.M., isn't it?"

My laughter stopped. "All right, I'm gonna say it now. You're pissed because you saw me making out with Lily-Ann at the pact party, right? Well, I'm sorry, but honestly, it was just one of those things that kind of happened, like when you made out with Sean Edwards. I mean Turquoise came in, and said the pact was over, anyway. And, see, I get that Lily-Ann is the daughter of the guy who hires you to clean his house, and now he's —"

"You don't get anything."

"What?"

"He's not that guy anymore," Megan said.

I knit my brow. I could hear her soft breathing on the other end. It sounded as if she were about to cry.

"He's not the guy who hires me to clean his house. He fired me."

"*What?* Why?"

"Because I'm not the only one who made out with Sean Edwards. It seems Jade made out with Sean Edwards, too. Only, *she* poached my keys from my skirt —"

"MILES!"

My mom threw my door open, baggy-eyed, wearing a ridiculous pajama combo.

"Hi, Mom," I whispered.

"Stop talking on your cell phone or we're confiscating it," she said.

"Okay."

Luckily, Megan overheard this fascinating bit of conversation. I knew she had, because she hung up before we could talk any further.

I was actually relieved.

All I needed was sleep and to pretend that this night had never happened.

Jade

I'd successfully spent Sunday in bed, pretending that I was *so* damaged from Lily-Ann Roth's punch that I couldn't possibly move (or help clean up).

Turquoise didn't utter a single word of protest. She just busied herself in silence — turning our little bungalow back into the immaculate home it would have been if Dad were there to supervise. She'd even gone to Clement's to pick up dish towels. But I couldn't tell if she'd done that just to make me feel worse. I sort of doubted it. Like Sean, Turkey was suddenly *cool*. Why the hell wasn't I? Her silence, in a way, was almost as disturbing to me as the fact that Megan hadn't answered or returned the five phone calls I'd made, or the one final desperate text.

meg, sorry & luv u. please forgive me for ruining ur summer. if u can.

I regretted pressing SEND as soon as I'd . . . well, pressed SEND. Of all the things I am least a fan of, in no particular order: 1) Evil spiked punch home-brewed by Miles's new tourist girlfriend, 2) Text shorthand, 3) Corniness, and 4) Lame apologies.

Sunday came and went without a peep from Megan.

Surprisingly, though, Sean Edwards called me. We'd said a stunned, awkward good-bye on Saturday night. But he called on Sunday to see how I was doing, and the sound of his deep voice and easy laugh instantly comforted me. And I found myself thinking, *Sean lives year-round in D.C. That's not so far. We could do weekends. . . .*

Then I got a grip. I couldn't date Sean, the tourist whom Megan had kissed. Things were feeling incestuous enough already.

When I got to the boardwalk on Monday morning, Miles was already there, tooling around on his skateboard. Aside from him, the boardwalk was deserted. I don't think I'd ever seen the sky so bright blue at this hour in the summer. There was a post-rainstorm chill in the air, too. It felt a lot more like October than July . . . fitting, I suppose. There's nothing like a little early fall depression to get the juices flowing. Miles wore a black Windbreaker and black wool cap, pulled so tightly over his blond hair that only a few wisps poked out from the back.

"Getting an early start on the day, are we?" I asked with big phony cheer. Dumb humor was about the only thing I could turn to at this point.

"Ha, ha." He didn't even look at me. He twirled once more on his board, and then kicked it up into his hands and turned toward the beach. The morning sun lit up his face like a giant golden spotlight.

"Okay, why are you so grumpy?" I asked. "You're the one with the hot new girlfriend, right?"

He whirled around, his jaw twitching. "She's not my

girlfriend. But I will say this: At least, we didn't break into her dad's mansion and have sex on their couch."

My stomach plummeted. "I did not . . . I did not . . ."

"Have sexual relations with that person?" Miles said. "Please, Jade, you're a lousy liar. Lying is not your specialty."

"Miles, please, let me just explain —"

"Explain *what*?" he shouted. "You stole Megan's keys and you hooked up with a lame tourist who you've been ragging on for your entire LIFE! And you got Megan fired in the process. Congratulations. I guess you really *do* hate this town."

My eyes began to sting. My throat worked convulsively, but I couldn't manage to swallow. "Miles," I gasped. "I feel like crap for getting Meg fired. But I didn't have sex with Sean Edwards. We made out a little, just like you made out with Lily-Ann. Also, Sean Edwards really isn't all that lame. He's a good guy. Really."

Miles blinked at me.

"What else do you want me to say?" I asked. I'd cried, or come close to crying, *way* too many times in the last forty-eight hours. "Megan offered me the keys, just so you know. Not that it's an excuse or makes anything better, but she told Sean and me to go to their house and watch *Twelve Apes*."

Miles cracked a grin and stared back out at the ocean. "*Twelve Monkeys*."

"Oh." I almost smiled. "Well, we never got a chance to watch the movie."

For a minute or two we were both silent. It actually could have been an hour, or it could have been fifteen seconds; whatever the length, it was excruciating. Then Miles let out a deep long sigh and tossed his skateboard back on wooden planks.

"You know, they really are tearing down this whole boardwalk," he said so quietly that I could barely hear him. "They're gonna build a dock that leads to a casino boat. They're gonna ruin all the surfing, so people can gamble instead."

I chewed my lip, resisting the temptation to reassure him that all this boardwalk stuff was just dumb gossip. "Is that what Lily-Ann said?" I asked.

"Megan. Last night on the phone. She said Roth was gonna make the announcement at Clam-Fest next month."

"Oh." A lone teardrop slipped down my cheek. I wasn't crying, though. Absolutely not. It was just the wind and the unseasonable coldness. I quickly wiped it away before Miles could see. "She told you this on the phone, after . . ." Again, I resisted a serious temptation to add: *After you smooched Lily-Ann Roth good night?* "Miles, there really is something I have to ask you. Did you *ever* tell Megan that we —"

"I didn't tell Megan anything. You know I wouldn't."

I nodded. "Got it." Well, this conversation had gone on about long enough. So I reverted to my usual M.O. I turned and ran away — Sarah-and-the-Jupiter-Bounce be damned. Why care about work? As far as summer jobs went, I was only good at getting myself or my best friends fired. Miles didn't call after me. As my flip-flops slapped the boardwalk, I only prayed that Turkey would still be asleep, so I could crawl into my cozy little shell of a bed.

Turquoise was awake.

Of course, she was. She was slurping coffee at the kitchen table, glued to her laptop, with a bunch of thick law books strewn everywhere. She'd go blind if she kept staring at that screen eighteen hours a day. Which it seemed she already had, given her new penchant for hideous secondhand skirts and tie-dyed concert T-shirts.

"What are you doing home?" she asked. "Don't you have work?"

I slumped into the chair across from her. "What's the point of working?" I lay my head on the table, burying my face in the crook of my arm. "They're gonna tear down the boardwalk, anyway. I figured I might as well say good-bye to the Jupiter Bounce now. Less painful that way."

"Jade, are you okay?"

"Fine," I mumbled.

"Jade, look at me."

I lifted my head. "What?"

Turquoise shoved her laptop aside and gave me one of those annoying, smarter-older-sister stares. "What's going on? I mean it. Something just happened. What is it?"

"How do you know?" I asked.

"Because I am your sister," she said simply, as if she'd read my mind.

For some stupid asinine reason, that made my throat tighten all over again. I resumed my ostrich-in-the-sand, head-in-arm slouch. "Miles and I got into a fight."

"About the party? About breaking the pact?"

I wasn't quite sure how to answer that. It *was* about all that, but in other ways, it wasn't about that at all. It was about Miles and me, and how we had this secret that we were still keeping from Megan. "Sort of," I mumbled. "I don't even know. I got Meg fired, and he's really pissed off about it."

"Jade, you did not get Megan fired," Turquoise soothed.

I raised my head again. "I broke into her employer's home and made out with her gardener on their couch — oh, while under the influence of alcohol. Those are the facts, Turkey. You lawyers *do* have a keen eye for the facts."

Turquoise laughed. "Those actually aren't the facts. At least, not all of them."

"You want to explain?" I asked, and I meant it. At this point, even a lecture from Turquoise would be tolerable, if only to ease my shattered conscience.

"Megan told you to take the keys. I heard her. Your going to the Roths' was *her* idea."

I hesitated for a moment. I tried to replay the series of events, but most of it was lost in the red haze of that punch. I guess I remembered, though, that Megan *had* said that Sean and I should watch the movie (whatever it was called) at the Roths' because the house was empty.

"Let me ask you something else," Turquoise continued. "Creating the pact? Whose idea was that? It wasn't yours, was it? It was Megan's."

I frowned. "Yeah. I guess so. She said she wanted all of us to spend the summer bonding, because it would be our last summer together before college."

Turquoise reached across the table and laid a hand on my arm. "Jade, when was the last time Megan made a grand pronouncement like that?"

"What's that supposed to mean?"

"She didn't want Miles to hook up with anyone," she whispered. "And I'm sure Miles didn't want anyone to hook up with *her*. Why do you think she ran off like that on Saturday night? She saw Miles with Lily-Ann. It was too much."

I leaned back in the kitchen chair, more baffled than I'd been all weekend. "Too much for what? Turkey, this isn't an episode of *Law & Order*. Stop playing an attorney for once and just actually spell it out."

"Fine." She pursed her lips and stood to refill her coffee cup. "Megan is in love with Miles," she said. She poured from the pot in the machine, and then blew on the steaming mug, studying it as if it held the secrets to the universe. "I don't blame her. If I were five years younger . . . but whatever — the point is the only time Megan ever steps up is if Miles is in danger of hooking up with someone. You're competition, too, you know that? I bet you didn't. That's why she wanted you to leave with Sean Edwards. She and Miles are meant for each other. They always have been."

I gaped at her. "Are you on drugs right now? Seriously. What's in that coffee? Megan is *not* in love with Miles. Nobody is meant for ANYBODY."

Turquoise just smiled in that extremely irritating, condescending way she has. And doubt started to creep in.

"Maybe," I murmured.

"Oh, Jade?" she said.

"Yes?" I didn't turn around.

"If you really did quit, you might want to use your spare time to clean up a little."

"Clean up? This place looks like it's been disinfected by a surgical team." I marched toward my room. "Nice job, by the way," I added grudgingly.

"You're welcome. And I'm not saying you have to clean up right this second. I'm just saying in general over the next few days. Until Thursday."

I paused in the narrow hallway. "Why? What happens Thursday?"

"Oh, that's right. I forgot to tell you since you were such a wreck yesterday . . . but Dad called. Nana's coming up to visit for Clam-Fest. We'll do the usual downtown dinner thing, but she'll be spending all next weekend with us. At least, she'll be able to stay in Dad's room this time. I know you get bummed when she stows her slips and bras in your drawers."

Now *that* was a sexy image.

I slammed my door and crawled into bed, shutting my eyes. I deliberately avoided looking at all the dumb, goofy photos of Megan and Miles I'd taped to the wall or thumb-tacked above my desk. This was supposed to be *our* summer. Where had it all gone wrong?

Megan

I had a fairly sleepless night, I have to say. Not that it mattered. I didn't have to show up anywhere Monday morning, so I might as well have stayed up. (Mom caught me in front of the TV at seven A.M. in my sweats. She left without even saying good-bye.) I was watching *Wolf* — an awful movie about werewolves, even though it does star Jack Nicholson. Yes, I suppose that's the one benefit of insomnia and unemployment for that matter: You can catch up on all the movies you haven't seen at least a dozen times.

By noon, though, the novelty had begun to wear off. I considered taking a nap. I decided against it. My eyes kept wandering to my cell phone, sitting on the side table like some kind of cursed amulet. I knew I'd have to call Jade at some point or reply to her text . . . but not right now. I just didn't have the energy for something that intense. Weirdly enough, what I wanted to do most was apologize to Lily-Ann. I knew enough about her family dynamics to know that she'd catch a lot of crap from her dad (and total silence and absence from her mom) — and the whole thing really *was* my fault.

Screw it. Just another unpleasant task that needed to get done. No worries; I used to clean houses for a living. I reached for the phone.

It rang before I could grab it.

ROTH, read the caller ID. Second time in thirty-six hours!

Nice. Perfect. Maybe he was planning on suing my mom and me for damages done to his couch by Jade and Sean? I shouldn't have been so quick to turn down Jade's offer of all her earnings. . . .

"Hello?" I answered.

"Megan?"

"Lily-Ann?"

"I'm just calling you to say that I am so, so sorry about everything that happened Saturday night. My dad is an asshole. Well, you already know that. But you're so better off not working for him. Besides, why does someone as smart as you clean houses for the summer? You should be working with Jade's sister at a law firm or something."

I rubbed my left temple with my free hand.

All at once, I had a migraine. The longer Lily-Ann jabbered on and on, the more she sounded like Jade: relentless and nonsensical. I'd reached a crisis point. The neuroses, the talking, the mercurial behavior, never any steadiness, anywhere, anytime, the way a true friend should be —

"Lily-Ann?"

"Yes?"

I collapsed back onto the couch.

"Why did you really call me now?"

She sighed apologetically. "See, I told you you're smart. I have some news. I . . . I . . . well, I guess I should just spit it out. My dad is taking your mom and me out Thursday night, downtown, to talk about the big Clam-Fest announcement. I said I wouldn't go if I couldn't bring a date."

"So why don't you invite Miles?" I asked, almost out of some bizarre instinct. (Actually, I knew the instinct; if she invited Miles, then I'd know he would be there and I wouldn't have to obsessively wonder if they were together.)

"Um . . . because I'd rather go with you. No offense to Miles."

I rubbed my temple again, feeling a *ping* of relief. "I don't understand," I said.

"I came to Seashell Point to cause trouble, Megan," she said in a hushed tone. "I told you that. My dad has been riding me all summer long about not making the 'right' friends in this town. He actually said that I should go to some random party hosted by these lame boarding-school kids three houses down because I was getting too comfortable with the 'locals.' And here he is, presenting himself like the biggest, best local around."

I shook my head, remembering the way he'd shouted at me on the phone. "I think this is a really bad idea, Lily-Ann. I mean, I appreciate that you called —"

"Of course, it's a bad idea!" she said gleefully. "What have I been trying to tell you? Besides, what do you have to lose? You've already lost your job, right? At worst, it's a free meal with your mom, some jerk who wants to rip down the boardwalk, . . . and me."

I chewed my lip, clutching the phone and staring into the blank TV. I don't think I'd ever heard her sound so plaintive. The problem was, Lily-Ann Roth was just a little too unpredictable — a hybrid of much too phony and much too real — and generally wrong at the wrong times.

But considering how pissed at Jade I was, maybe Lily-Ann was my one friend left.

There was a beep.

"That's my other line," I said. "Hold on one sec."

"I'll let you go," Lily-Ann murmured. "Just think about it, all right? Call me when you can, but definitely before Thursday. Bye."

"Okay." I clicked over to call-waiting. "Hello?"

"Meg?"

I swallowed. *Oops.* I really should have broken the habit of not checking the caller ID. I'd been way too distracted this summer.

"Hey, Jade."

"Did you get any of my messages?" she asked breathlessly.

"I did," I said. I gazed into the TV screen again, my warped reflection staring back at me, fish-eye-lens style. I wanted to shout at the top of my lungs, *Did you ever think I might be mad on some level that you hooked up with Sean, too?* (Not true, but still, it would make her feel guilty.) *And why am I mad at you? Do you really think I care about losing my cleaning job? Or does it still come down to the same stupid issue? That I'm jealous of how you and Miles have always been so comfortable together? How do you do it? What's your secret? Can you share it with me?* The one question that finally popped out of my mouth, though, was: "Hey, how come you aren't at work right now?"

She laughed softly. "That's funny. Turkey just asked me the same thing."

"And?"

"Well, I decided since you didn't want my money, I wouldn't work, either. I'm quitting my job. Like I said, there isn't much point in taking tickets at the Jupiter Bounce if there isn't gonna be a Jupiter Bounce anymore."

"What did Sarah say?"

"Uh . . ." Jade clucked her tongue. "Actually, I haven't told her yet. I was hoping my absence would speak for itself. You know, like Brian Ashe's absence did, when he dropped out of school for a month last year? Anyway, knowing Sarah, she'll probably get a job running this casino boat or whatever it is. Can't you see that?"

That wasn't funny. Not in the least. But still, I cracked a smile and chuckled. "I hate how you always do that," I heard myself say.

"Do what?"

"Make me really mad at you one second, and then make me laugh the very next."

"Well, I'm trying to fix the first part, if that's any consolation," she said. "Besides, your two cutest expressions are those of furious rage and wanton hilarity."

I sighed. "Well . . . thanks."

"So am I forgiven?" she asked.

"In some ways, yes," I answered. I stood and walked to the drawn shades. It looked gorgeous outside. I needed some fresh air. "So what are you doing today, anyway? Maybe we should go surfing. We're both unemployed."

Jade laughed. "I would, but it's too cold. Plus, um, neither of us ever surfed before. We could ask Miles to teach us, but he still has a job. Plus . . ."

I pictured Miles teaching us to surf. I pictured him finally giving up his fear of the water, and throwing that stickered skateboard aside, and taking out his surfboard and wet suit again. I pictured the three of us in the ocean — the way it used to be — with Jade and I just standing at the water's edge, letting the tide roll over our bare feet, watching Miles paddle out to catch the next big wave.

"Hey, Meg?" Jade asked.

"Yeah?" I struggled to snap out of my moronic moment of nostalgic reverie.

"That's not all."

"That's not all of . . . what?"

She clucked her tongue again, a little more loudly. "Um — Nana is coming to town. And here's the thing. She's coming on a Thursday night. So that means she'll want to take Turkey and me out to dinner. And she'll want to invite you and Miles, too, since she's known you guys forever." She cleared her throat. "Will you guys please come to Rupert's for dinner with Nana and Miles and Turkey on Thursday night?"

The migraine returned, full-force. *Rupert's with Jade's Nana . . . and MILES.*

Now that I was jobless, I couldn't imagine spending an evening downtown at the fanciest and most overpriced seafood restaurant in town (and, I might add, the one most shamelessly geared toward tourists). It also didn't help that the Seashell Point Tourist Board was on that same quaint, cozy, cobblestone block.

But I had an excuse.

"Actually, and I know this is going to sound weird, but I have dinner plans that night with the Roths and my mom," I said.

"Are you *serious?*" Jade asked. I could tell by her voice that she was smiling. "That's great! I mean, if the Roths invited you to dinner, it means they can't be too pissed off about the whole me-and-Sean thing, right? Whew. Yes, please, by all means — absolutely. You are excused. Hit it. Where are you guys going?"

I thought for a minute. I thought about what Jade had asked, and what Lily-Ann had asked. And I knew with twisted certainty (the kind that only comes from sleeplessness and misery) that there was only one way to bring Miles in on the action, which he absolutely needed to be in on.

"I think we're going to Rupert's," I lied. "But here's a crazy idea. How about we all go together?"

"I love it," Jade said.

Miles

"**A**re you out of your mind?"

Megan laughed.

"No, seriously." I fought to keep the cordless phone balanced between my cheek and shoulder blade — dumping out the millionth batch of sizzling clams with one hand into our sink, while wiping the sweat from my brow with the other. (Donny had taken a "sick day.") At least, there was a weird summer cold front. If you want an idea of the temperature inside Sonny's Clam Shack, take a reading of whatever it is outside, be it 60 or 103, and raise it 30 degrees. "You're asking me to go to dinner with Jade, and Jade's grandma, Jade's sister, and you, your mom, Lily-Ann, *and* her parents? At Rupert's? Who's gonna pay for *me*?"

"Maybe I will," a grown-up voice said outside the booth.

I dropped the fryer back into the fry pit.

Some of the burning grease splashed onto my apron. Great. Well, at least this wasn't the first time this summer I felt like Megan, only in guy form.

Mr. Roth stood before me in his classic getup: rolled-up seersucker pants (only this time with white tennis shoes), blue button-down shirt with rolled-up sleeves, and a sun hat. He probably owned forty versions of the exact same outfit. He must have, because he looked impeccably coiffed and crisp every single afternoon.

"Don't mean to surprise you, just a little early today," he said with a disarming smile. "How ya doin'?"

"Miles?" Megan's tinny voice asked in the earpiece.

"Can I call you back?" I whispered. "I have a customer."

"Sure, I'm sorry. But think about it. It really could be a great way for all of us to get through this weirdness and patch things up —"

I shut the phone and jammed it into my apron pocket.

"Hello, sir!" I said. My voice cracked twice in three syllables. I rubbed my palms on my pants. I tried to smile, shifting from foot to foot. "The usual? A two-dollar bucket?"

"You know, clams are slang for dollars, too," he said, reaching into his pocket and forking over two crumpled bills. "Did you know that, Miles?"

I nodded. "Yeah. I did. There are bunch of stores down at the south end that use that same exact joke . . . you know the south end of the board . . ." I decided not to complete the sentence. I whirled around and snatched a cup, scooping up the hot clams from the sink just like I'd scooped up cups of punch on Saturday night —

"That's a soda cup, Miles," Mr. Roth said. "I'd like a bucket. Unless you've changed your policy?"

"No, sir!" I laughed again. I didn't sound like a laugh; it sounded like the Jupiter Bounce cushion when it cracks a hole. "I'm just . . ." I dumped the cup into a bucket, then immediately scooped out another, and another — until finally the bucket was spilling over. "Here. And you know what? Keep the clams, sir. Ha! Get it?" I shoved the dollars back toward him across the counter. "These are on me. I mean . . . you know, if you were serious about paying for me at Rupert's."

He stared at me, unblinking, a curious grin on his lips.

My heart thumped inside my chest.

"What would your boss say if you gave me a freebie?" he asked.

"Um . . . probably that you deserve it?"

He leaned across the counter, flabby elbows right on the grease stains, his craggy face a little too close to my own. (Also, now I realized he didn't look so much like a flabby George Clooney, but more like some dude who may have been good-looking once . . . a long time ago.) "Why would I deserve it?" he asked. "You can do better, Miles. Your boss is one of the most vocal protesters against my plan."

I straightened, fighting to smile with all my might. "What plan is that?"

"To replace this piece-of-crap boardwalk with a dock and floating casino."

"That's um . . . that's — I don't know. Grown-up stuff. But if you're a regular — I mean, you stop by literally every day — so . . . it's a Sonny's Clam Shack policy to give you a freebie every now and then. I'm sure Donny would agree."

Mr. Roth winked at me and grabbed the clams. He left the money sitting on the counter. He turned away, stuffing a few into his mouth, crunching loudly. "By the way," he said, still chewing. "I can't make it to Rupert's that night. Besides, the truth is, I prefer your clams to the gourmet stuff they serve there. But I'm sure you'll have a great time. My daughter is a big fan of yours. I guess you know that, though."

I wondered what it would be like to plunge my head into the deep fryer.

"Miles, I'm just busting your chops," he said with a light smile. He popped another clam into his mouth. "Have a good time Thursday night. And I'm sure your boss will come around. We're gonna need these clams on *The Royal We!*"

I watched, slack-jawed, as he waddled down the boardwalk, disappearing down the stairs at the very far end.

Then I yanked the phone out of my pocket and dialed Megan. Hooking up with Lily-Ann Roth had been the hugest mistake of my life. And — of course — whenever I make a huge mistake (say, breaking my leg on a surfboard in order to make Megan happy), the very first person I want to call is . . . well, you get the gist.

"Hello?" Megan answered in the middle of the first ring.

"All right, so Mr. Roth isn't coming Thursday night, and he also knows that I hooked up with Lily-Ann — not that it meant anything — or I'm pretty sure I think he does." It all came pouring out in a rapid breath, basically one long incomprehensible word.

"Um . . . hello to you, too, Miles," Megan said drily.

"Am I talking to Jade?" I asked. "This is serious!"

"I didn't say it wasn't. So are you going to come to dinner or not? I called to invite you to dinner, if you remember. So I think the fact that Mr. Roth isn't coming is a good thing. It is for me, anyway."

I glanced at the deep fryer. It was starting to sizzle again. And I still had a batch of clams in the sink. Why did Donny have to take *today* off, of all days? I tried to breathe evenly. "I . . . I guess I should come to dinner. I should at least talk to Lily-Ann and tell her that kissing her was a mistake. And that kissing . . ." I didn't finish.

Megan laughed.

"What?" I asked.

"I would think about how you want to phrase it. And, if you look back, it probably *wasn't* the biggest mistake you've ever made in your life. Not even close."

"What do you mean?"

A series of mistakes flashed through my head: Riding the wave that broke my leg and made me petrified of the ocean; giving up surfing; agreeing to work in this steaming hellhole of a clam shack for another summer; making out with Lily-Ann (not the biggest, agreed) . . . but kissing Jade. That was the biggest. And neither of us had told Megan. On the other hand, no: The biggest was basically making out with all the girls I *shouldn't* have been making out with for the last three years (some that are best left unmentioned) – and not making out with the one that I should have.

"Miles?"

"Listen, Megan . . ."

Before I could go on, a trio of twelve-year-old tourists appeared at the counter. All three were blonde. All were *way* underdressed for their age. They were pretty much younger clones of older siblings who'd collectively decided to strip down to their bikinis at the pact party.

"Hey, are you the guy who had that surfing accident?" one of them asked. The other two were whispering to each other and laughing. "I heard Cheryl Roth talking about it. You know, at the Lopezes' party down the beach."

Who are the Lopezes'? What kind of party were you at with Lily-Ann Roth's mother? I wanted to scold. *You should be at home rereading* Harry Potter!

"Miles?" Megan asked. "Are you there?"

"You know, I'm not even sure. I'd definitely rather be somewhere else. But in answer to your question — yeah, I'll come to dinner. Looking forward to it."

Then I turned to face the onslaught of tourists.

Jade

Imagine, if you will, an old woman who resembles Dr. Seuss's seminal character, Yertle the Turtle. The wrinkles, the hunched physique, but most of all — the total lack of chin. In other words, imagine a mouth and neck that seamlessly blend together. Now remove the shell and the lizard green. Substitute it for a leathery brown. Add some heft and some makeup and perfume, throw on a freakish Saks pantsuit — and make Yertle a biped instead of an amphibian.

Voilà! You have our nana. Mrs. Jessica Cohen. Or as she prefers, Mrs. Daniel Cohen, even though Grandpa (rest in peace) died long before either Turkey and I were born.

This was the figure who emerged from the cab in front of Rupert's that evening. The sun had set, the crickets were buzzing, the gas-lit streetlamps were flickering . . . and Nana's Saks pantsuit was Yertle-green.

"Hello, my darlings!" she cried, easing herself out the door as the cabdriver removed her luggage from the trunk. "I am never flying again!"

I blinked at Turquoise.

She looked pretty happy, which I couldn't understand, because tonight's roster at dinner might have been the most off-kilter posse ever assembled in the history of Seashell Point.

History, I repeated silently to myself, with a twinge of

anxiety. Yep — there was a lot of history waiting inside: Miles, Megan, Ms. Kim, and Lily-Ann. Turquoise was a walking artifact, herself, in a patchwork, button-down Granny dress. At least it wasn't a pantsuit.

"Why don't they pave these streets?" Nana asked. "I feel nauseous."

Turquoise swept forward and pecked her on the cheek, then grabbed her suitcase, leading her up the stairs. "Nice to see you. And the streets are paved, Nana. They're just paved with cobblestone. That's why they're so bumpy. You know that."

"What kind of outfit are you wearing?" she demanded. "You look like Jade."

I myself was in a peasant skirt and tank top. Now even I had to laugh. I pecked Nana on the cheek, too, holding my breath for fear of toxic perfume shock. "Thanks for coming to visit," I managed.

"Well, this may be the last time," she grumbled. I held the door open for her as she toddled inside, keeping her steady with my free hand. "The flight was delayed. The cab ride from the airport was more than an hour. I'm not even going to discuss what it cost. Why did your father have to settle here of all places?"

Turkey and I exchanged a grin. Rupert's was packed (as always), dimly lit in the classic overpriced fancy restaurant way, and just . . . pretentious. The rugs, the bow-tied waiters, the soft classical music and hushed conversations . . . at least there weren't any B-list celebrities there yet.

146

"No clams tonight," Nana announced, apropos of nothing.

"Why not?" Turquoise asked. She left the suitcase with the maître d'.

I clutched Nana's arm, keeping her steady. I stared at our table. Miles, Meg, Lily-Ann, and Meg's mom all wore the same stricken-but-polite smiles anyone would wear when a senior citizen in a green pantsuit approaches. Miles even stood and pulled out her chair. Which was extra nice, because easing Nana into it allowed me to take some focus off of Megan and Lily-Ann — both of whom had on black and spaghetti-strap dresses tonight. Apparently, their peas-in-a-pod vibe was back on. Fine. Tonight's dinner was about forging the peace among all of us. As far as I could remember, anyway. Or was it about me finding out if Miles had confessed to Megan what had happened between us, and my confessing that I thought I was starting to fall for Sean Edwards? No. Of course not.

"Ahh," Nana moaned happily, once she was ensconced. "This is nice. Except for the name of the place. What kind of name is Rupert's?"

I seized Turquoise's arm before she sat down. "Let's get her that first red wine," I whispered in her ear.

"But that just makes her more talkative," Turquoise hissed back.

"Only at first. Then she'll get really sleepy, really fast."

Turquoise waved to the waiter.

I sat and joined the awkward, silent smile-fest.

"What brings you to town this summer, Mrs. Cohen?" Megan's mom asked politely. She could always be counted on to break the ice. Of course, she could; she was head of the tourist board. "It's nice to see you again."

"It is!" Miles and Meg both agreed in unison. They looked at each other.

Nana lifted her shoulders. "I'm here because I had to check on my granddaughters, honey. Two wild girls, living on their own? When their father was the same age as Jade is now, you wouldn't *believe* the nonsense he was up to. A mother knows, though. A mother knows. *Ah-mein.*"

Lily-Ann laughed. "Did you just say . . . ?"

"She said Amen," I translated.

"*Ah-mein.* I have an accent. What are you gonna do?" Nana said.

"Um . . . nothing. I'm Lily-Ann Roth by the way." She stood and extended a hand.

Nana waved her back down with her gnarled fingers. "Nice to meet you, honey, but don't bother with the formalities. Handshaking is off limits, what with the arthritis." Just then Turquoise returned with a glass of red wine. For the first time all night, Nana smiled, too. She lifted the glass and cheered all of us.

Some highlights of the ensuing hour-long horror show:
- Nana spent fifteen minutes arguing with the waiter about whether the chicken was "very, truly thoroughly prepared. I don't want trichinosis."

- Lily-Ann kept making flirty eyes at Miles, which he took great pains to avoid. Megan's skin grew increasingly pale as her conversation grew increasingly nonexistent.
- Megan's mom chose dessert to make the big announcement: Come Labor Day, demolition would begin on the boardwalk, and by Memorial Day of next summer, Seashell Point would have a splendid new faux-wood dock, an "extension of Main Street, straight from the library to the floating casino!"
- On the plus side, Ms. Kim also insisted on paying for the entire meal.

Okay, I said to myself, surreptitiously eyeing everyone's dessert plates. *Five more minutes, tops. Ms. Kim will ask for the check, and we'll all be able to flee.*

Miles was the first to speak up. "Well, I probably should be on my way," he said. He shoved a last little bit of chocolate cake into his mouth and dabbed his lips with his napkin. "I don't mean to be rude, but my parents are expecting me home by ten o'clock."

It occurred to me that I hadn't seen him wear a jacket and tie since my bat-mitzvah. But it suited him right now, especially with his floppy blond hair.

Nana grinned crookedly at him. "Dear, how long have you been living here?"

Miles shrugged. "Um, my whole life —"

"You know, my son has been living here for thirty-three years. Thirty-three! The man is an overgrown teenager! But, God bless him, I understand why he came. The boardwalk. I think it's a shame you're going to build a dock, even though I like boats. But every resort town has gambling. Every resort town is the same — you got your Saks, your Gucci, your Prada . . . it doesn't matter where you are. You could be in Bali. What I'm saying about the boardwalk is that at any time of day, it's such a nice thing to be able to walk out and see the kids, and smell the cotton candy, and watch all the young deviants out on the waves . . . I don't mean to offend anyone here."

"I agree with you, Mrs. Cohen," Megan murmured — in almost the exact same voice she'd used when she'd said that she wanted to be mayor of Seashell Point, way back in the fourth grade.

"The dock will be a vast improvement, I assure you," Ms. Kim stated with a terse smile. "It will be safer, and —"

"Safer?" Miles interrupted. "What about the surfing? That'll be a lot more dangerous with a big thing sticking out into the water." He paused again, his eyes still glued to Megan's. "But maybe you're right," he said.

"So, Miles," Nana said.

"Yes, ma'am?"

"When are you and Megan going to get married?" she asked.

Megan's mouth fell open. Miles's eyes bulged, but his smile remained intact.

"Nana!" I shouted.

"What? *You* can't marry him, sweetheart. He's not Jewish." She nodded toward Lily-Ann. "And Miles can't marry this one. She's a summer girl."

I shot a horrified glare at Turquoise. I considered bolting — anything but to look at Miles and Megan, who'd both begun staring down at their half-eaten plates of cake, faces bright red.

Lily-Ann was laughing hysterically.

And, of course, Megan's mom was stone-faced.

Turquoise started laughing, too.

I blinked several times. Then I started laughing. There wasn't much else to do.

"What's so funny?" Nana asked.

"You are," I muttered.

Well, not really. Okay, Nana *was* funny — but what was funnier: She was absolutely right.

It hit me then. Hard. *Of course.* Megan and Miles.

Miles and Megan were better for each other than Miles and I ever could or would be. They *were* actually meant for each other. It was another one of those epiphany moments, like realizing that fixing a screen door and buying the right brand of bug-repelling scented candles *are* sort of crucial to growing up. My heart leaped as a series of obvious revelations clicked into place. It was as if I'd suddenly been handed the teacher's edition to a trig exam. I think Lily-Ann must have seen it, as well, because the flirt light went out in her eyes. We even traded a strange little grin across the table. The answers were all there, plain as Megan's pink cheeks.

Megan and Miles both love weird movies. Megan and Miles both love cheesy downtown Seashell Point. Megan and Miles both love the boardwalk. . . .

And I was wrong about something else. There *was* something to do. I could stop running away for once. Better yet, I had an idea about how to start.

"Well, I guess I'm just a big, silly old comedian then," Nana said. "Or *yenta*? Nah, that means matchmaker. No matter. I think we're all done here, yes?" She waved a hand at the maître d'. "Check, please!"

Miles

After all the drama of loading Jade and Turquoise and their grandma into a Seashell Point taxi, of uncomfortably hugging Lily-Ann good night, and shaking Ms. Kim's hand trying to remain poised and holding my breath . . . after all *that*, I found myself standing in front of Rupert's, alone with Megan. The whirlwind was over. I loosened my tie and breathed a very long sigh of relief.

"Where do you think Lily-Ann went?" Megan asked, squinting toward the boardwalk. "You think she'll be okay getting home?"

"She's definitely somebody who knows how to take care of herself," I murmured. "She probably kicked off her heels and started running as fast as she could."

Megan laughed.

"What?" I said.

"You really wanted to get out of there, huh?"

"You didn't?"

"No . . . I did. I was just . . ."

"You were just . . . ?" I prompted.

"I was impressed with how you handled my mom. She was being really rude. That was a weird dinner. I was impressed with how you handled everyone, actually."

I took a second to consider my dinnertime behavior. It didn't seem terribly impressive to me. I'd basically kept quiet the whole time, except to ask lame polite questions. I'd tried not to look at Lily-Ann. That was something, I supposed. I'd also managed not to fight with Jade, even though I'd been *extremely* tempted, as she'd set the weirdness in motion in the first place.

"Well, thanks," I said. "But I didn't do much. We all went in there knowing it would be weird."

"Yeah, but you were the only one who was himself the whole night. Or, I guess Jade's nana, too. I don't think she's ever had a phony moment in her life."

"You think people were phony? Your mom sure wasn't."

Megan bowed her head. "I don't want to talk about it. She bums me out."

"Hey, look, why don't I walk you home?" I suggested. "We can take the scenic route. The boardwalk. What do you say?"

Tonight is the night, I thought. *If I'm not going to be phony, I should tell her what happened with Jade. It's only right.*

Without even so much as a nod, she took my hand in hers and pulled me down Main Street — toward the boardwalk. We'd never held hands before. But it felt right. It felt more than right . . . It felt natural and electric and focusing, so maybe it wasn't strange at all. I couldn't help but glance over my shoulder, sizing up all the little details of downtown: the lit-up quaint storefronts, perfectly manicured strips of lawn, the wrought-iron lamps, and town houses. It all suddenly looked fake. If they tore down the boardwalk, what next? Rip up the cobblestones and tear down the two-hundred-year-old landmarks? Cut down the trees? Replace Rupert's with a Wal-Mart?

"Miles?" Megan whispered.

"Yeah?"

"What are you looking at?"

"Nothing," I muttered.

I shook my head and picked up my pace, tugging Megan toward the official Seashell Point boardwalk entrance. A three-foot-tall bronze statue of a clamshell stood at the center of the broad stairwell. All of us locals had been tempted to deface it at one point. (Brian Ashe actually had. He'd spray-painted a big, crooked smiley face.) But I couldn't help but think of Jade every time I laid eyes on it. *"What sort of a place uses a clam as its mascot?"* she would joke. *"I mean, think about our stupid school. We're the bulldogs. And even WE'RE more creative. Besides, bulldogs can always be cute, furry stuffed animals . . . not some weird metal monolith."*

Again, I felt mad at her. But it wasn't that . . . that was just Jade-talk. It was the secret. I couldn't keep it to myself anymore. Megan deserved to know. It was the only way I could finally feel healed after everything — *truly* healed.

Megan let go of my hand when we reached the railing.

Neither of us spoke for a bit.

I shivered. There'd been a thunderstorm this afternoon. A crisp ocean wind washed over us. The tide lapped the beach in a gentle rhythm.

"You know," Megan remarked in a faraway voice, gazing

up at the night sky, "Right after the rain, you can really see a lot more stars."

I guess she was right. But I'd never really looked at the sky. I always looked at the water. I missed those waves. Even the ones that were small and low — just perfect enough for a beginning surfer to find balance — like I had, a long time ago. I could run home, grab my board, and find my legs again. Right this second. I cast a sidelong glance at Megan. Her eyes were still on the stars. She was hugging herself, her arms glowing in the moonlight.

"Hey, are you cold?" I asked. I wriggled out of my dumb jacket. "Put this on."

She grinned. "Miles, that's sweet, but you don't need to loan me your blazer."

"You actually think I want to wear this thing?"

"Ha!" She grabbed it from my hands and slipped it on. The sleeves hung over her arms. It was weird . . . I mean, we were both about the same height, but now I knew how much more slender she was than me. "Thanks," she said, wrapping the floppy sleeves around herself. She turned back to the ocean. "Maybe I'll find you a conch shell out there for show-and-tell. You know, to return the favor."

"No problem. Honestly, I hate that jacket. It's tweed."

"Miles, how come you don't surf anymore?" Megan asked suddenly.

I froze. "Huh?"

"Seriously."

"What do you mean?"

"You ride that skateboard Jade got you, which is great, but why don't you surf? Your leg is pretty much healed, isn't it? The guys from *Dogtown and Z-Boys* kept surfing, even though they skated. And some of them got hurt, too. Remember?"

I turned away. "I don't know. My leg hurts when it rains," I mumbled, and I was telling the truth — even though it was painful. I had to keep telling the truth. *Tell Megan now,* my crowded head shouted. *Tell her about what happened with Jade and that you only made out with Lily-Ann on a stupid meaningless whim.*

"You can keep walking me home though, can't you?"

I swallowed and nodded.

Her black eyes glistened in the night. I stepped an inch closer.

I wanted to kiss her so, so much.

"Miles I really want —" Her cell phone beeped. "Ugh," she groaned. "I'm sure it's my mom, *demanding* to know where I am. I did make a mental note to check my caller ID, so I could screen . . ." She dug her phone out of her handbag and frowned.

"What?" I asked.

She wrinkled her forehead and shoved the phone against her ear, locking eyes with me. "Jade?" she answered. "What's up?"

For a second, I felt like grabbing the phone out of Megan's hand and hurling it into the surf. And then it hit me. I wasn't mad at Jade. I was mad at me. I should have never kissed her or Lily-Ann . . . I shouldn't have; I shouldn't have. . . .

"You what?" Megan asked into the phone.

What's she saying? I mouthed silently.

Megan shrugged. "She wants us to meet her and Turquoise at the library tomorrow at ten. She told me to tell you to take a 'Donny sick day.' The sisters are cooking up some scheme." She paused for a second and then laughed. "Okay, whatever. Bye, Jade." She dropped the phone back into her bag and slung it over her shoulder.

I scratched my chin. "Jade and Turquoise are doing something together?" I asked. My brain was suddenly *too* crowded. I'd reached a critical overload. "What *happened* this summer?" I asked Megan.

Megan laughed lightly. She took my hand again. "Nothing. So are you gonna walk me home, or what?"

"Well, since I don't have my skateboard, I guess now there's no excuse not to."

We strolled the length of the boardwalk, our fancy shoes clackity-clacking. We walked past all the closed stands and shops — past the petting zoo, past the Amusement Alley Jupiter Bounce, past Sonny's . . . then past all the surf gear stands, where the haggard old metal dudes sold their wares for "clams" . . . until we reached the end, where the stairs led down to the beach right in front of the Roths' back door. Without a word between us, we took off our shoes and socks and dashed down the stairs, running through the cool sand. Once we were a good long distance from the Roths', we continued to walk the beach in silence — hands still held, her heels in her free hand, my stupid scuffed shoes and socks in mine. We laughed for no reason.

I had no idea what time it was, how much time had passed.

And then we were almost at the burned-out Seashell Point lighthouse near Megan's home. The lighthouse was dark, but the Kims' house was brightly lit, as bright as the Roths' mansion — perched on the rocky bluff nearby. I paused on the beach to catch my breath. I thought about inviting myself inside and confessing. I thought . . .

"Miles?" Megan asked, still holding my hand.

"So I guess this is where you turn off and climb up to the end of Ocean Avenue," I said, sounding like an idiot. "I guess."

Look how beautiful she is in that dress. It's ridiculous. This is like some horrible cheesy soft-rock ballad. I could write the lyrics right now: "The ivory skin and the long black hair" . . . Jesus. I should use this opportunity to kiss her. We've never been closer than we are right now. I should —

"You guess what, Miles?" Megan asked, snapping me back into reality.

"Megan, there's something I've wanted to tell you ever since . . . you know, my accident," I said. "Well, I guess about since about a month after the accident."

"Yeah?" Her black eyes drew closer to mine.

"I — um, well, something . . . I guess — something happened between Jade and me," I stammered. "I don't know what it was, but . . ."

Megan stepped back, letting my fingers slip away. "But it was something?" she prodded. Her voice dropped lower than I had ever heard it.

"Yeah. I don't know." I glanced back toward the dim lights of the boardwalk. "She came over to fix me lunch that first day back from the hospital, and I guess we were just both so happy to see each other, and she gave me that skateboard . . . I don't know."

"You don't know *what*?" she demanded.

"We sort of made out."

The worst part? I'd always imagined it would feel so great to come clean. As if it would magically lift this burden from my shoulders or cure the pain in my leg. It didn't. Instead, I felt like *more* of an idiot. I stared down at my dress shirt and rolled-up suit pants. I *looked* like an idiot, too.

Megan shrugged as if she didn't care one bit. "So you've made out with both Lily-Ann and Jade." Her tone was hard. "No worries. Anyone in Seashell Point you haven't made out with?"

"Come on, Megan, please —"

"Good night, Miles."

She turned and vanished up the path to her house.

Seconds later, I heard her front door slam.

She still had my jacket on.

Part Five
Show-and-Tell

Jade

Should I have invited Sean Edwards to our library rendezvous? Probably not. But Nana's words had been ringing through my head all night. *"Yenta. That means matchmaker."* And every time I thought of that, I thought about kissing Sean Edwards. And then I thought about how right Megan and Miles were for each other — and how I'd never noticed the obvious.

As Turkey and I hurried down the boardwalk to the library, we passed the Jupiter Bounce. I stuck to the railing, just in case we happened to spot Sarah. It was Friday and I hadn't been to work all week. Sarah hadn't called. I took her silence to mean that she'd no longer require my services. I was used to getting fired. And that was all right, because I was entering a new profession: *Yenta*.

Turkey rounded the corner and down the steps onto Main Street, hurrying toward the redbrick Victorian — turret, porch, and yes, even rocking chairs — that served as the Seashell Point Library. It may not have housed a lot of books, but at least it had a functioning air conditioner. And, as a handwritten sign taped to the front door boldly proclaimed: INTERNET ACCESS FROM IO A.M. TO 2 P.M.!

"You know I'm starting to understand why you've been working at home all summer," I mumbled to my sister, clambering up the porch stairs behind her.

She shoved open the big, creaky wooden door. Instantly, we were assaulted by the smell of mothballs.

Megan, Miles, and Sean were already there. Or I guess a more accurate description would be: They were the *only* ones there. Except for Ms. Fitzgerald, the bespectacled librarian. The three of them sat at the end of the big, long oak table in the center of the room, the one with the big, clunky, old desktop computer, circa 1998, that offered the library's prized "Internet Access!" for four hours a day. Megan and Miles were, for some reason, avoiding looking at each other. And when I smiled at Megan, her eyes were like ice. At least, Sean seemed happy to see me.

"Hey, guys," I said brightly. "You're probably wondering why I asked you all here. Well —"

"*Shh!*" Ms. Fitzgerald and Turquoise hissed at the same time.

Neither Megan nor Miles nor Sean replied. They were all stone-faced. Turquoise sat at the computer and logged in. So . . . my big plan for easing any possible tension might have been better prepared.

"Actually, I am," whispered a voice from the stacks.

I whirled and spotted Lily-Ann Roth thumbing through some dictionary-size textbook in the row of REFERENCE shelves.

"You're what?" I asked. *Tension factor = quadrupled.*

"Wondering why you invited everybody here." She snapped the book shut. "I mean I'm sorry I crashed, but Sean told me."

"Sean told you?" I whirled at him. I tried to frown. I couldn't. He shrugged, fiddling with his necklace. He was wearing some ridiculous band T-shirt, too. I hated that he looked cute.

"That you were having a little social activist powwow," Lily-Ann murmured. She delicately slipped the book back on the shelf and stepped toward me. "I thought I might be of service."

"How's that?"

"To stop my father from destroying the boardwalk."

"Go on," I encouraged.

"What do you think *I* think about the boardwalk?" Lily-Ann asked me. Her tone lay somewhere between curious and accusing.

"How should I know?" I asked.

"All right," Sean said. "I invited Lily-Ann here because I went over to her house this morning to . . . you know, apologize for what happened with Jade and me in the house" — he coughed, pretending to watch whatever Turquoise was doing on the computer — "but her dad wasn't there. So I apologized to her, and we got into a talk, you know . . . about the town and the people in it and she said wanted to help."

I tried to keep on my game face, but I broke into a smile. "That's sweet!"

Sean looked confused. "It is?"

Both Miles and Megan leaned back from the table and frowned at me.

"What, you don't believe him?" Lily-Ann asked.

"*Shh!*" Turquoise and Ms. Fitzgerald hissed again.

I shot a sympathetic grin at Lily-Ann. Not only did I believe Sean (he was a little too uncomplicated to lie, God bless him), but I believed *her*, too. "Maybe I'm wrong," I interjected. "Maybe Sean has a point here, guys. Maybe Mr. Roth's daughter, Lily-Ann, wants to help out the friends she's made this summer —"

"Ha!" Megan barked.

"What?"

"Jade, you are so full of crap."

Either Megan had been replaced with an alien . . . or, I didn't know. "I'm full of crap?" I asked, knowing she was right.

"Yes."

"Well, I'm sorry," I muttered. "But I've wanted to tell you for a long time now —"

"About what? How you suddenly love Seashell Point and want to save the boardwalk? Or how you accidentally made out with Miles?"

My heart stopped.

"Well, yes." My mind went into the self-defensive comic mode it usually does when stress reaches a critical mass and I want to crawl into a hole. "Both. Forgive me, for I have sinned."

Megan's and Miles's faces might have been carved in stone: THE MOUNT RUSHMORE OF PISSED-OFF SEASHELL POINT LOCALS.

"Speaking of accidentally making out," Sean said, "And this probably isn't the best time to bring it up, but why did you guys decide to have that no-hooking-up party in the first place?"

I nodded toward Megan, who I was hoping was still my friend. "You'll have to ask her. It was her idea —"

"Oh, my God, this is so beautiful!" Turquoise interrupted in a whisper, her fingers still feverishly clattering on the keyboard. "I think we can win this thing!"

"You do?" Miles asked under his breath.

"Yes! The town has an ordinance that forbids pollution of the beach 'to protect the shellfish population.' It's right here." She jabbed at the screen, beaming up at us.

I honestly don't think I'd ever loved Turkey more than at that moment. (Then again, I'd barely even *liked* her until that moment. Not that the two really have much to do with each other — "like" and "love," that is. After all, I loved Nana and I still wanted to strangle her every single time I heard her wheeze.) But our little conversation about the no-hooking-up pact party had reached its limits, and Turkey came through.

"What's right there?" Megan asked. She leaned over and squinted at the screen, her face still about a zillion shades of red. I knew we'd have to have a real talk later.

"In 1966," Turkey proclaimed, reading from whatever obscure article she'd conjured, "the incorporated town of Seashell Point voted to institute a ban on toxic waste in excess of one gallon per day within a quarter mile of its beaches to protect its swimmers and surfers."

None of us said a word. I glanced at Sean. He looked as confused as I felt.

"Um . . . ?" I finally asked.

Turquoise laughed. "Can you imagine how much waste a floating casino dumps into the water every *hour*?" she replied. "I'm serious. Where I go to law school, these huge cruise ships always float by, and you can see this evil stuff just *pouring* out."

"Okay, okay, we get the picture," I muttered.

Megan chewed a fingernail. "So what are you saying, exactly?"

"I'm saying that the citizens of Seashell Point have already decided that they don't want anything like a floating casino near their beach. And the best part: It's law. It's been voted on. So he can't do this. The deal is illegal. It's democracy."

"An illegal deal — like the pact party?" Megan asked flatly.

Sean grinned. So did Miles.

"Well, you know what Winston Churchill said," Turquoise remarked.

"Turkey, how the hell would any of us know what Winston Churchill said?" I asked.

"'Democracy is the worst form of government, except for all the others that have been tried,'" she quoted, a mischievous sparkle in her eye.

I pretended to stick my finger down my throat. Lily-Ann rubbed her hands together, her expression even more wickedly delighted than my sister's. "You guys should totally call my dad on this at Clam-Fest. You should bring it up there. He's always talking about stupid crap like the law and democracy. This would be the biggest slap in the face, at a town celebration."

Ah-mein, I wanted to say.

"What's so stupid about the law and democracy?" Sean asked.

"Lots," Lily-Ann replied. "Anyway, when did you get so deep?"

"Yeah, when did you?" I marveled. The words just sort of popped out. Then I remembered myself. I blinked at Sean.

I can't believe I just said that. I am the biggest jerk on the planet.

"Jade, quit while you're ahead," Turquoise advised.

"Quit while you're behind," Sean chimed in.

I scooted next to him and pinched his arm. I'm not sure why. I suppose I wasn't thinking. But he did smile. So I guess I had that going for me. What I didn't have going for me was that I'd failed miserably as a *yenta.*

Miles

Jade and Sean decided to stay with Turquoise at the library to prepare a "cheat sheet." Turquoise explained it as such: She'd pass around a bunch of leaflets before Clam-Fest. We'd all position ourselves in strategic locations to heckle Lily-Ann's father with horrible facts about how his casino boat would poison the waters.

The world truly is turning upside down, I kept thinking. *Jade and Turquoise are suddenly acting like sisters. Sean Edwards suddenly has a brain, like Scarecrow from* The Wizard of Oz. *Megan hates my guts. And Lily-Ann . . . is glancing at her watch, even though she claims she's all for the heckling. Unsurprisingly, she splits to go shopping.*

"See you tomorrow, guys!" Lily-Ann called, pumping a clenched fist in the air. "Give my father your very worst!"

Megan frowned. She hurried out the door with a cursory wave at the rest of us.

I hurried after Megan.

That left Megan and me alone, outside on the boardwalk once again . . . a mere twelve hours after we'd embarked on last night's disastrous walk.

"So, um, can I get back my blazer?" I asked.

It was a weak question, but it broke the painful silence. I wrapped my arms against my body, even though it was seventy-five degrees and totally cloudless.

Megan smiled wistfully.

"Megan? My jacket? It's my one nice coat. I sort of need it."

"I think I like the sight of you hugging yourself. It reminds me . . ."

"Yeah, it reminds you?"

"That you like to hug yourself," she finished.

"Who doesn't?"

Megan laughed.

"Go on," I prodded. I prayed that I'd cracked her armor.

"I'm talking about how you and Jade wrap yourselves up in these cloaks of —"

"Of what, Meg? You wrap yourself up in a cloak of silence! And Jade . . . I mean, neither of you are huggers! And neither am I. But it's like, you're always hugging. You two have an invisible hug on at all times. And that's cool."

"An invisible hug?" Megan quipped, in what might have been an attempt to sound like Jade. "Is that like a wig or a toupee?"

"Don't," I snapped. "I'm serious."

Megan backed away. "Miles —"

"Don't 'Miles' me. I'm sick of this crap. So give me a hug, Megan. Give me a hug right now. But hug me like you mean it. Hug me like you invisibly hug Jade. Hug me like you *mean* it."

She stared into my eyes, her long black hair flapping in the morning wind. "What do you mean, how I mean it?"

"You know exactly what I mean."

Megan did hug me like she meant it. I felt her hug down the whole length of my body. I could smell her sweet skin. We clung to each other.

When I finally opened my eyes, Megan was gazing back at me.

"What?" I breathed huskily.

"You know . . . that time I made out with Sean Edwards in the haunted house?"

I withdrew from her embrace. "It's not really a sight I enjoy remembering."

"Well, you should," Megan stated.

I should. I should . . .

"Jade was on a break from the Jupiter Bounce, and you were on a break from Sonny's," she went on. "And you two were off to the side, watching us and laughing and all cozy . . . I'd just hit that point — I'm going to pull a Jade here and say something really uncomfortable — I'd just hit the point where I'd stopped being the gangly, pale, tall geek and turned into something else. And Sean Edwards asked me to take the ride with him."

"Megan —"

"No, no, just let me finish." She stroked my hair with her fingers. "I did it because I was trying to make you jealous."

I thought for a moment . . . and then I stopped thinking.

I put my hands on Megan's waist and pulled her close to me, kissing her. I took every second to savor the way she felt pressed against me, the way her lips perfectly melted into mine. The kiss was warm and sweet. Hot. I was surprised, in the best possible way, when she touched her tongue to mine. Our breathing quickened. This was nearly a decade in coming, but the wondrous magical moment had finally arrived —

And then my cell phone rang.

We stepped apart. It was Jade.

"Hey!" she said.

I gulped, staring at Megan as she rubbed her lips. "Uh . . . hey."

"Hey, are you with Meg right now?" she asked.

"Yeah?" I said.

"Can you put her on?"

"Uh . . . sure." I handed the phone to Megan.

"Yeah, Jade?" she said. At first, her face was a blank slate, but then she was laughing out loud. "Perfect! You have my blessing. Thanks for thinking to give the heads-up." She hung up and handed the phone back to me.

"What was that?" I managed, my pulse still racing.

"Jade thought about putting a giant clam next to Mr. Roth in his bed, to get rid of him. You know . . . like they did in *The Godfather*? With the horse head?"

"Ha! That's brilliant."

"Actually, I have a better idea." She stepped forward, put her hands on my cheeks, and kissed me again.

"That is a better idea."

"No, there's something I have to do," Megan breathed into my ear. "I have to do it for me. I have to see if there's another way around Turquoise's heckling plan. I also have to see if Mr. Roth will forgive me —"

"Forget it."

"Forget what?"

"I want you to stay here with me. This will sound as stupid as the old Sean Edwards," I said. "But I really love you. I mean like . . . *love*, love you."

Megan pressed her lips against mine again before I could make a further ass of myself. Then she turned and hurried off down the boardwalk. This time, her silence was exactly what I needed.

Megan

I felt reborn. I was glowing, trembling, laughing to myself. *Miles kissed me.* Miles *KISSED* me.

That was all that mattered. I wasn't even nervous as I knocked on the door of the Roth's rent-a-mansion.

Mr. Roth appeared in his signature getup. Only this time, he was holding a drink with a little umbrella. It wasn't even noon. He gave me a quick once-over, and then scowled. "Lily-Ann isn't home."

He nodded toward his wife. It occurred to me that I'd never seen Mrs. Roth speak unless she had a cocktail in her hand, either — of the martini variety. She didn't have one now. Only he did. Naturally, she turned and scrambled up the stairs.

I did the best I could to force my lips into a smile. "I totally understand and appreciate that, but I'm not here to see Lily-Ann. I'm here to see you. I want to apologize for what happened with Jade Cohen and Sean Edwards. I just want you to know that —"

"I'm glad you stopped by," Mr. Roth interrupted. All at once, his demeanor changed. His jovial laugh was back. "I mean that."

I peered at him as he ushered me in. I couldn't quite bring myself to cross the threshold. "You're . . . glad?" I asked.

"Yes. I was just on the phone with your mother, so I know that she knows I have no idea that you're here. It took some initiative on your part to come down here and offer your apology on your own. And I appreciate that. I truly do." He rattled his ice cubes at me and then plodded down the hall toward his magnificent beachfront living room, his bare feet smacking the tile. "And I'd like to apologize to you for yelling at you the way I did. Let's sit on the deck. You want a glass of soda or something?"

"Can we just talk here?" I asked.

He paused and turned back toward me, frowning curiously. "Sure."

"I . . . um . . . I also just think that this boardwalk idea is wrong," I said. "I think you should look a little more at the town's history first and what people feel."

Mr. Roth nodded and leaned against the wall. He took a long sip of his highball. "Megan, I was like you when I was younger, too. And someday you're going to learn what's right, as opposed to what you think is right."

"Wrong."

His smile vanished. "I beg your pardon?"

"Jade swiped those keys from my skirt. But I egged her on. That's why I'm still apologizing. I'm responsible."

His face darkened. He jerked a finger toward the door. "I don't know why you stopped by, but please get out. I'd prefer not to see you again unless your mother is present."

"Fine." I shook my head, my heart racing, and marched

toward the door. "But you should try saying 'sorry' for once in your life. It might feel good."

"You expect me to believe that?" he barked after me.

I paused at the knob and turned. "Of course not. You've never said sorry."

He twisted his lips. "Not about that. About this egging this girl on to steal your keys from your skirt?"

"It's the truth." I yanked my cell phone from my pocket. My hand was trembling. "Call her right now. Ask her what happened. Do it."

He didn't answer.

"It doesn't feel good to be told what to do," I said. "Does it?"

"No," he said, turning his back on me. "It doesn't. Not by a —"

I slammed the door.

I called Jade first.

"Psst, Jade?" I whispered.

"Why are you whispering?" Jade asked.

"I'm calling from outside Clement's." I'd run there, because it felt like a safe haven.

"Why?"

"It doesn't matter! Just throw your sister's cheat sheets away, all right? I'll do all the talking tomorrow at Clam-Fest. It was my mom who made this . . . this . . ."

"Faustian bargain?" Jade suggested.

"Exactly! Mom made this pact with the devil, and it's up to me to fix it. And that's exactly what I'm going to do." I stopped talking. I was practically panting. I could feel my heart thumping in my chest. "Jade? Are you there?"

"Yeah, I'm here. I'm just shocked. And proud. Why?"

"Because I want to be mayor of Seashell Point, remember?"

"Of course, I remember," Jade said gently. "It's just that you should be saying all this to Miles, not me. That's just my opinion. You know, as a . . . *yenta.*"

Now I was silent.

"Meg?"

"Yeah?"

"Have you told Miles?" she asked. "About saving the boardwalk?"

I swallowed. "Not yet."

"Well, he's the one who should really be hearing this. I'm just your old buddy who tries to get you to take care of your skin. Which reminds me, be sure to wear plenty of sunblock tomorrow. Pick up some extra at Clement's while you're there —"

"Jade?" I said, and I could feel a huge smile breaking across my face. "I kissed Miles. Or he kissed me. I don't know."

Jade laughed softly. "You don't know, huh?"

My smile faded. "Jade . . . I really *don't* know. I mean, what happened between you and Miles . . . I wish you had told me. I wish he had told me. I know you never knew I had feelings for him — and, yeah, of course I do — but it still hurts like a mother to imagine you guys —"

"Meg, I feel terrible," Jade interrupted. "You don't know how sorry I am. I wish I had told you right then. I just felt so awkward about the whole thing. I think I thought it was best to pretend it had never happened. But the last thing I'd ever want to do is hurt you. You're my . . . my other half. The sister I always wanted to have."

My throat tightened. I wasn't sure what to say.

"And that was last summer," Jade went on, her voice plaintive. "And we were all messed up from the accident. It didn't mean much beyond that."

"I know," I whispered. "You're the sister I always wanted, too."

"Meg, you know what's weird?" Jade asked.

I could think of a thousand possible responses to that question. So I decided to keep my mouth shut.

"Here's what's weird," Jade went on. "We don't hug that much. And we're best friends. We should hug more."

I swallowed, laughing as my eyes moistened. "I fully agree."

There was a pause, but not an uncomfortable one.

"Are you okay?" I asked quietly. "About me and Miles —"

"Meg, if you and Miles get together, then all will be right with the world. Even if the boardwalk does get torn down."

And just like that, I knew she was right.

Jade

Clam-Fest morning, Turquoise and I decided to go for a long swim in the ocean. I needed to clear my head, but I felt so much freer now that my secret was out in the open. If only I could calm my nerves. The water was gray and rough, like a certain morning last August. Bad omen? When we came back, we made breakfast. Nana was still asleep. But we were out of orange juice. "Don't worry. I'll go to Clement's," Turquoise said.

It was only then that we discovered the note on the front-hall floor, scribbled in what looked like lipstick, over the back of one of Turquoise's law printouts.

> *Darlings,*
>
> *My arthritis is acting up so I left. I should have said good-bye, but my return flight is at 3:19 P.M. Monday. I wanted to catch the Saturday 5:23 A.M. instead. I don't have to pay extra if I get to the airport on time. I understand there's some kind of procedure with the ticket lady. I don't much care for this town. Awful thing to say, I know. Your father is upset with me, too. Did I already tell you that? He should get a haircut. He's flying back soon. I can't remember the date.*
>
> *Love, Nana*
>
> *P.S. Thank you for a wonderful visit. Never take me back to that restaurant.*

I stared at Turquoise.

Nana had been gone for nearly four hours, and we hadn't even realized it. We both rolled on the floor in hysterics for about the next twenty minutes. It helped.

Megan

" **I** still don't know about this."

There we stood, Miles and me, in the midst of the enormous crowd on Main Street. Luckily, it was packed so tightly that we were able to hold hands without anybody seeing . . . although, I suppose that proverbial cat was out of the bag by now.

Nearby stood Jade, Turquoise, and Sean Edwards. When we'd met up that morning, Jade and I had hugged — a real, tight, you're-my-best-friend-and-life-preserver hug. We needed that.

Now Jade and Sean weren't holding hands, but they weren't exactly *not* holding hands, either. I could feel the spark between them from where I stood. Maybe being in love makes you more attuned to other people being in love. Or, at least, in like.

I couldn't believe that my mom and Lily-Ann's dad had decided to make the announcement in the exact spot. I mean, it was right next to the giant bronze clam statue — where Donny would usually have sparked up a giant outdoor grill to hoots and hollers, kicking off Clam-Fest. The sad part was that all us Seashell Point locals knew Clam-Fest was nothing, just an annual excuse to bring even *more* people to the boardwalk. (Actually, in addition to preparing my cheat sheet about the true boardwalk facts, Turquoise did some other research. The tradition started because June 23 was supposedly the day of the year when there were the most clams on the beach. I imagine this tradition started with drunk or hungover surfers.)

"You don't know about what?" Miles asked.

"My plan."

"You'll do great." He kissed my cheek. I wondered when Miles's kissing me was ever going to *not* make me grin from ear to ear and blush. Possibly never.

Mr. Roth stepped to the small wooden podium, dressed in his perennial seersucker-blue-shirt combo — though this time, he'd added the jacket to the suit pants as well. He tapped the microphone: *Tat-ta-tat. Tat. Tat.* The sound echoed across the loudspeakers mounted on either side of him. My jaw tightened. The guy even had the nerve to co-opt Donny's signature mic tap — the one he always gave before kicking off Clam-Fest. (The opening clap soundtrack to a seventies song called "Car Wash," which was also the theme song to a seventies movie about community involvement. Not that Arnold Roth would have the slightest clue about that.) Crime upon crime . . .

"Megan?" Miles whispered.

"Yes?"

"Shut this idiot up." He kissed me lightly on the lips. He took my shoulders in his hands. "You can do it," he whispered. "This is what you were born to do. When you were a kid, you said you wanted to be mayor of Seashell Point, remember?"

"Miles, I —"

"GOOD MORNING, SEASHELL POINT!"

Mr. Roth's voice thundered across the crowd. There were a few scattered claps, but not many. Mom stepped up beside him (clad in pearls and the smart pink Donna Karan suit, of course) and clasped her hands behind her back with the phoniest smile I'd ever seen. And speaking of mayors, the *real* mayor — Evan Wells — was nowhere to be found. Who takes a vacation from a resort town during the height of the season? Oh, right . . . Evan Wells, the one local who somehow managed to buy property in five other states. Maybe going after his conspicuous absence would be my next civic project.

"Happy Clam-Fest!" Mr. Roth continued. "Today, however, in a break of tradition, I am pleased to announce that Clam-Fest will begin on the beach outside the house I've rented this summer — a lovely house in a beautiful town. Please bring your appetites. The nice part is that we'll be able to walk the entire length of our boardwalk. . . . A little exercise always encourages an appetite. Ha!"

Nobody laughed. There were a few hushed murmurings. Miles took my hand again and squeezed it.

"Now . . . I'm happy to announce that Seashell Point has made a bold decision," Mr. Roth went on. "It's one that will not only benefit its citizens and visitors in the short term, but make Seashell Point, truly, THE premier East Coast hot spot in the long term. As I've maintained ever since I've chanced upon your lovely town, the boardwalk, while aesthetically beautiful, isn't safe. Its support beams are rotting.

Accidents happen as a result of surfing. . . . In a word, the boardwalk is *unsafe* — and let's be honest with ourselves: outdated. It's time to bring in a breath of fresh air."

I held my own breath. I think Miles was holding his breath, too.

"Now, imagine, your boardwalk on the water," Mr. Roth plowed on, "*truly* on the water, a floating palace with all that the current boardwalk has to offer — and I mean that sincerely — all the games, shops, restaurants . . . and yes, even a petting zoo and a haunted house." He chuckled to himself again. "Now, I am happy to take any questions, because I'm sure you have some."

Miles nudged me in the ribs.

My hand shot up.

Mr. Roth grinned at my mom. "Yes, Ms. Kim?"

"What's your favorite food?"

Mr. Roth laughed. His eyes roved the crowd, deliberately avoiding mine. "Clams, darling. Any other questions?"

"No, seriously — just work with me here for a second," I called back.

A few people turned to me. I could feel Jade's eyes on me, which made me feel better. I yanked Turquoise's cheat sheet out of my pocket and held it in front of my face. The sheet rippled. But I couldn't tell if that was because of the breeze or because I was so nervous. Maybe it wasn't such a great idea to rely on the cheat sheet. I knew it by heart anyway. "Let's take clams. Do you think it's okay to eat fried clams every day of the week?"

"What?"

"You swing by Sonny's Clam Shack almost every afternoon to order a two-dollar bucket, do you not?"

"Well, yes. I enjoy the —"

"Now let me finish," I interrupted. "I'm sorry. But you know what the health hazards of eating a bucket of cheap fried clams every day are?"

His face reddened. He shot a quick glance at his wife. "Yes, but I don't finish the bucket. I just nibble on a few. It's not that big a deal."

"Maybe not. But we have the statistics, care of certain concerned citizens. Grams of fat, and this is trans fat, mind you — forty-five per serving. Cholesterol: I can't quote the number here, for decorum's sake." I glanced up from the paper. "Should I go on?"

"I'm in the middle of an important civic announcement," he said.

"Right. You're breaking the law."

"Pardon?" he asked.

"Let's get back to the clams. Hypothetically? Say we make up a little story with a tragic ending. Say you come to Sonny's Clam Shack, and you nibble on clams every afternoon — and then you drop dead on the last day of the summer from clogged arteries."

"Young lady, please. That's not funny. That's sick."

"I agree completely. But my question is, would it be fair to say that Miles and Donny, those who sell you the clams, are in any way responsible?"

He smacked the podium with his fist. "Of course not! I would never —"

"Exactly!" I shouted over him. "Because eating clams is *your* choice. You *choose* to poison yourself with that luscious, deep trans-fat flavor. I don't blame you. I would eat a bucket of fried clams every day, too, if I could."

Miles's grip tightened on my fingers. Some people clapped and laughed.

"Will you get to the point?" he snapped. "You were my maid, for the love of God. I'm in the middle of something here."

At the word *maid*, everybody fell into a strange catatonic silence.

It was a bit surreal, almost magical. But in that silent split second, it was as if all the self-righteous tourists and the self-righteous locals had magically joined forces. *Maid* was a term nobody used anymore ... was it? I held Turquoise's cheat sheet in front of my face with my still trembling hand, keeping my other hand firmly clung to Miles's.

My mom fidgeted beside Mr. Roth on the platform. She finally cleared her throat and stepped to the microphone. "Megan? You were saying?"

"Yes, I was saying ... your casino boat, *The Royal We*, when it's idle at the dock, will still dump more than ninety gallons of waste in the water per day. I'm not talking just gasoline, either. I'm talking *human* waste. The gasoline is far over the limit, too, but that's a whole other issue. You see, this is where all of us locals will still be swimming and hopefully surfing. Seashell Point local law specifically states that no more than one gallon of waste be deposited within a quarter mile of the beach. You know, in the late sixties, they even set up a perimeter of buoys to demarcate the 'safe' zone for dumping waste. Mr. Browning and Donny have both provided affidavits." I dug the other papers out of my back pocket and waved them in the air, along with the cheat sheet.

"This is all very interesting," Mr. Roth said, his voice echoing through the loudspeakers. "I still don't understand what you're trying to tell me."

"I'm telling you that there won't be a dock. The boardwalk will stay."

"And I'm telling you that *you're* a smart, idealistic – if somewhat naive – high-school girl with no idea of what she's talking about. We've signed contracts."

I laughed. "Great. Then you're going to jail. Mom?"

The collective gasp in the crowd grew louder. I tried to ignore all the stares. I tried to focus on Miles's hand. I focused on the reassurance of his skin pressed against mine.

Mr. Roth turned to my mom again. He cupped the microphone, whispering something in her ear.

"Excuse me, Mr. Roth!" Sean yelled from the audience.

I burst out with a grin.

"Yes?" Mr. Roth said, uncovering the microphone.

"So . . . like . . . Let me get this straight? You have this mansion with a greenhouse. I mean literally like a biosphere — and I know, because I was the gardener. It's totally enclosed and protected and everything — what I mean to say is . . . you'd be willing to dump toxic waste and fecal matter onto our beach, but keep your little garden safe?"

At that point, pandemonium erupted.

Jade

I wasn't sure what was going to happen. I guess nobody was. I gave Sean a kiss on the cheek, snaked my way through the bewildered, angry crowd, wishing Dad were here. He'd love this! It was a real-live protest rally. Or the closest thing in Seashell Point anyway. . . .

A hand tapped my back: *Tat-ta-tat. Tat Tat.*

I spun around.

It was Miles. He'd never looked happier. I peered over his shoulder.

"Crazy, huh?" I asked. "Where's —"

"Megan?" he interrupted.

I stopped standing on my tiptoes. "That's the one."

"She bolted with your sister to talk to her mom. They're not gonna let Roth go through with it. I saw Lily-Ann chasing after them, too."

"That's . . . awesome." I fell back on my feet.

"Thanks," he said.

I stared at him for a long time. He *was* gorgeous. No doubt about it. Anybody with hair that blond and eyes that brown couldn't *help* but be gorgeous. But he looked better than he had in a year. He'd get back to surfing, too. I knew he would. Megan would help him.

"For what?" I managed at last.

"For Megan."

I swallowed. *No more crying.* "Well, it's best for you. And for her."

"It is?"

"Miles, you know my nana was wrong. The reason I can't marry you is not because you're not Jewish."

He laughed, those irreplaceable bright brown eyes twinkling. "It isn't?"

"No. It's because you want to be a giraffe when you grow up. I need someone with longer-term prospects. Now, Meg — given her height, she needs a giraffe."

"So where does that leave you? Say . . . with a certain handsome tourist?" he whispered conspiratorially. I laughed.

Sean Edwards was kind of a brand-new wild card. Or not. Maybe he was just a cute boy I'd kissed.

Miles and I hugged. "That's 'certain handsome *gardener*,' to you, buddy," I whispered back.

"Well, you have my blessing," he said.

"And you have mine."

"*Ah-mein*," he said.

I slapped him lightly on his tousled head. He didn't seem to care. He hurried back through the crowds and over to Megan, who blew me a kiss. I knew then that Miles would be all right from now on. We all would. Even in the middle of a Seashell Point riot.

Take a peek at another fun summer read by Erin Haft:

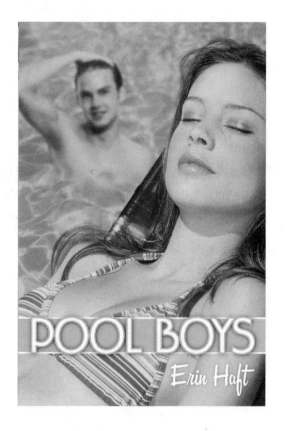

Dive right in ...

Welcome to the exclusive Silver Oaks Country Club, where scandals, secrets, and forbidden hookups are part of the lush scenery — along with all those beautiful boys and girls.

Charlotte was the first to jump in the pool.

Bad move. She immediately resurfaced and splashed around for a minute, her teeth chattering. *CO-O-O-LD!* After a few sputtering gasps, she brushed her soaking red hair from her eyes and launched into her breaststroke, even though she hated that word. She thought about her breasts (or rather, the lack thereof) way too often.

Charlotte von Klaus had been the first to do lots of things. She'd been the first to make out with a boy (Caleb Ramsey, in sixth grade, in a game of Spin the Bottle that had gotten slightly out of hand); the first to sneak into the downstairs sauna at Silver Oaks (on a dare from Brooke); and the first to take a slug of very pricey Pinot Noir straight from the bottle (after her parents' divorce last year. Luckily, with some brute force, Georgia had managed to wrestle the bottle away from Charlotte and toss it in the recycling bin).

And she was the first of her friends to see a therapist. And still the only one.

The way Charlotte saw it, if you were the first to do something, then you carved out some quality alone time — even if you were in the company of your two best friends. Or, even if you were in the company of a boy. After all, she hadn't been thinking about Caleb Ramsey when she'd made out with him. She'd been thinking about her math homework, and walking Stella McCartney — the von Klaus family's smelly (male) Labrador — and which *South Park* rerun would be on that night.

So as Charlotte plowed through the icy water, kicking her legs and paddling, she didn't think about swimming. She thought about Marcus Craft.

Out of the corner of her eye, she could see him. Due to the overabundance of chlorine, he appeared extra fuzzy and dreamlike. He was still languorously draped over the side of his chair, chatting up the Hot New Girl who had somehow snuck in under the radar. How had none of them heard of her before today? Even Ethan Brennan knew about her. It was absurd.

Breathe, stroke, kick . . . Breathe, stroke, kick . . . Breathe, stroke, kick . . .

Actually, what was more absurd was that Charlotte had to practice swimming.

For reasons never made clear, Old Fairfield Country Day — otherwise known as the Tombs (Charlotte coined the moniker herself after a freakish school trip to Washington, DC, but that was a very long story) — required that their students pass a swimming test in order to graduate. This was now the summer before senior year, and Charlotte was in big trouble. Brooke and Georgia would have no problem. Brooke had been a pool girl since birth. And there wasn't a single sport Georgia couldn't master. Give her a bow and arrow; she'd become an archery champ in days. Hence, all of

Charlotte's friends would say good-bye to the Tombs and attend college, whereas Charlotte envisioned herself flunking out and spiraling downward in a self-destructive binge of steak sandwiches until she became a grotesque tabloid headline:

1,543-LB WOMAN IS NEW GUINNESS WORLD RECORD HOLDER FOR FATTEST HUMAN. "CAN'T LEAVE BED!!!" SHE SAYS.

Breathe, stroke, kick . . . Breathe, stroke, kick . . . Breathe, stroke, kick . . .

Charlotte reached the shallow end and nearly bumped her head on the stone steps. *Ugh.* She was about as graceful as a squid. Was Marcus watching her? She hoped not. On the other hand, if she started to drown, then Marcus would have to dive in and rescue her. But on the third hand (was there a third hand?), that would violate the Second Unspoken Rule of Silver Oaks, which Charlotte had written herself:

Thou Shalt Not Poach Thy Friend's Love Interest.

Brooke was clearly interested in Marcus. Though that didn't mean that Charlotte couldn't still check him out. Their parents surreptitiously checked out their friends' significant others all the time, after all. It was the adult thing to do.

"How's the water?" a boy's voice asked.

Charlotte shook out her soaking red hair and turned to see Caleb Ramsey standing poolside, frowning.

Good lord, did that boy need some sun. As always, at this time of year, his lanky body was even whiter than Brooke's, especially in contrast with his oversized, dark blue swim trunks and his mop of black hair. And as always, at this time of year, he somehow still managed to be completely adorable.

"Freezing," Charlotte said. "It's like *March of the Penguins* in here."

"Seriously, C."

"I am being serious. The good part is, much like said penguins, I have lots of blubber to keep me warm." Charlotte leaned against the side of the pool and rested her chin on her dripping arms, smiling up at him. "Unlike you."

"Will you do me a favor?" Caleb asked, returning the smile. "If you ever fish for a compliment again by claiming to be fat, will you give me permission to chop you up and bury you on the golf course?"

Charlotte stood up straight and saluted, deliberately splashing water on Caleb's knees. "Permission granted."

"Hey!" He laughed and scooted away. "Damn. That *is* cold."

"Once you're in, it gets better. I'm gonna do one more lap. My shrink says exercise is good for me." She launched into the water again.

Charlotte hadn't been able to joke around about therapy at first. She hadn't told Brooke and Georgia that she was even *seeing* a shrink until after her second session, post-divorce last year. Not because she was worried they would think she was a loon (they already knew that), but mostly because she wondered if they'd be hurt. After all, who needed a shrink when you've shared everything with your two best friends since the age of diapers?

Surprisingly, Brooke had been the first to speak up. "I think this is exactly what you need to do, sweetie," she'd said, squeezing Charlotte's hand. (This from the girl whose tenth-grade yearbook quote was: *"Life is far too important a thing to talk seriously about."* — Oscar Wilde.) And Charlotte began to realize Brooke was right. The difference between best friends and therapists? Best friends could and should constantly surprise you. Therapists couldn't and shouldn't. Dr. Gilmore was no exception. He'd worn the exact same paisley bow tie to every single session, now going on number fifty-four.

Charlotte reached the shallow end again, allowing her feet to touch the pool floor. She rubbed the water from her hair and eyes. Caleb was staring at Valerie now, though pretending not to. And Brooke was pretending to read *Elle*, and pretending not to watch Valerie and Marcus as well. Georgia was hurrying into the cabana to change, obviously about to meet Ethan on the tennis courts.

Caleb crouched down beside Charlotte, sitting on the edge of the tile and sticking his feet into the water. He eased them down very slowly, up to his knees, and then cringed, as if it were torture.

"You really are a wimp," Charlotte teased.

"Well, not all of us can be lifeguards." His voice dropped to a whisper. "By the way, have you met . . . ?" He didn't bother to finish the question.

"Sort of. I said hello to him, anyway. I still have yet to say hi to *her.*"

Caleb glanced up at the lifeguard chair, and then returned his gaze to the water. He kicked his feet absently. "She seems pretty cool."

"Really? Have you talked to her?"

"No. This is the first time I've seen her."

"Easy there, Caleb. You're drooling."

"That's because of *you,* Charlotte," he said, rolling his eyes. "You know, I still haven't gotten over that game of Spin the Bottle."

Charlotte laughed in spite of herself. "Funny. I was just thinking about that."

"You were?" He puffed out his skinny chest. "I was that good, huh?"

"Don't flatter yourself, stallion. Actually I was thinking about how when we made out, you were the *last* thing on my mind."

"Thanks," Caleb said flatly. "I appreciate it."

"I didn't mean it like that. I was just thinking . . . I don't know."

"Very articulate," he mused.

"Hey, go easy on me. I got a C-minus in English this year."

"It's not your fault. You had Mr. Lowry. The guy's a sadist."

"No kidding," she grumbled. Charlotte stretched out and kicked her feet to keep warm. "Anyway, enough about the Tombs. It's summer. No school talk."

"Agreed. May the Tombs rest in peace. So what's with Brooke? She seems bummed."

"I think it's because —" Charlotte bit her lip. She was about to say: *This new girl is stealing her thunder,* but that wasn't fair to Brooke. Besides, Brooke may *not* have been bummed, she may have been deeply involved in an article in *Elle*, a brilliant piece about the "25 Most Creative Ways to Wear Swarovski Crystals!"

"Because of what?" Caleb prodded.

"Because Ethan said the three of us are like a street gang," Charlotte replied, mostly because it was the first thing that came to mind.

"You're a lousy liar, Charlotte von Klaus," Caleb said with a laugh.

"He did say that!" she insisted, trying not to smile. "What? You don't believe me? Ask him."

"No, I believe you. And I agree. I'd say you three are exactly like a street gang. Except, you know, that you're socialites from Connecticut who spend all your time at the country club. That's the only difference."

"Is that what you really think of us?" She stopped kicking and stood, rubbing her wet arms. She wasn't sure why, but Caleb's jab had struck a chord inside her.

"Actually, no, I think that's what everyone else here thinks of you," he said, withdrawing his feet from the water. He made air quotes. "'Brooke, Georgia, and Charlotte,'" he proclaimed in a deep voice. "'The Princess, the Jock, and the Clown.'"

"Oh, God," Charlotte murmured, aghast. "That's even worse! Who thinks that?"

"Nobody. I'm kidding. If anything, *you're* the princess." He stuck his big toe in the water and splashed her playfully. "Look, I should run. I have to escape before my parents get here. Are you gonna be around later?"

Charlotte nodded. She shivered and stared at the sunlight sparkling off the tiny pool waves.

"Hey, are you all right?" Caleb asked. "I was just messing around."

"I know, I know." She pushed back into the water. "I'm just in a weird mood. I guess we all are. End of school and all. And in August we're getting officially inducted into Silver Oaks, and all that crap." Silver Oaks policy dictated that when members' kids turned eighteen — as Charlotte, Caleb, Brooke, and Georgia had — they were inducted as official members of the Club, complete with a glam, glitzy ball and freakishly stuffy "ceremony."

"Yeah, well, welcome to my world," Caleb said wryly. "The world of weird moods." He sighed and turned, disappearing into the pool cabana.

Charlotte watched him go. What was she so upset about, anyway? And why should she care what anybody said about her and her friends, or, least of all, care about Caleb Ramsey?

Maybe because she was scared that this summer *was* going to be more of the same old, same old. More hanging out by the pool. More of the same old banter with the same old pool *boys*: Caleb, and Ethan, and Robby Miller —a recent Old Fairfield Country Day graduate — arrogant and in training to be a frat boy this fall. And Robby's fratty friends, Mike and Johnny and Billy, who were all pretty much interchangeable, and were also headed off to college at the end of the summer.

So maybe it was time to mix things up a little. Maybe somebody just had to make the first move.

Charlotte leaped out of the pool and marched right over to Marcus and Valerie, dripping water on the flagstones.

"Hi, again!" she said. "You're Valerie, right? Great to meet you." She extended a wet hand. "I'm Charlotte von Klaus. C for short. Welcome to Silver Oaks."